Twisted Affection: How Love Can Break You

Morgan B. Blake

Published by CopyPeople.com, 2024.

Table of Contents

Silent Control 1
Gaslighted 5
The Financial Trap 9
Bleeding Heart 13
The Perfect Life 18
A Perfect Lie 22
The Cost of Saving Her 26
The Green-Eyed Shadow 30
The Hollow Comfort 34
The Price of Silence 38
The Quiet Collapse 42
The Price of Devotion 46
Torn Threads 51
The Weight of Her Love 55
The Quiet Heart 59
The Chains of Affection 63
The Final Choice 67
The Lies We Live 71
The Ties That Bind 75
Only Me 79
The Weight of Her Words 83
The Only One Who Cares 87
The Wedge Between Us 91
Unraveled 95
The Price of Love 99
The Walls Between Us 103
The Thin Line Between Love and Control 107
The Invisible Standard 111
The Perfect Lie 115
The Isolation Project 119
The Cost of Care 123

The Weight of Love	127
The Strings You Pull	131
The Fall and Rise	135
Fractured Mirror	139
The Silent Betrayal	143
The Fabricated Truth	147
The Weight of Silence	151
The Mirror's Edge	155
The Price of Affection	159
The Illusion of Choice	163
The Space Between Us	167
The Price of Praise	171
Under the Surface	175
Under Her Thumb	179
The Race to Nowhere	183
The Weight of Her Care	187
The Illusion of Love	191
The Empty Promises	195
The Cost of Love	199
Get Another Book Free	203

Created by the CopyPeople.com[1]
All rights reserved.
Copyright © 2005 onwards.
By reading this book, you agree to the below Terms and Conditions.
CopyPeople.com[2] retains all rights to these products.

The characters, locations, and events depicted in this book are fictitious. Any resemblance to actual persons, living or dead, events, or locations is purely coincidental. This work is a product of the author's imagination and is intended solely for entertainment purposes.

All rights reserved. No part of this book may be reproduced, stored in a retrieval system, or transmitted in any form or by any means—electronic, mechanical, photocopying, recording, or otherwise—without the prior written permission of the publisher and the author, except in the case of brief quotations embodied in critical articles and reviews.

The views and opinions expressed in this book are those of the characters and do not necessarily reflect the official policy or position of the author, publisher, or any other entity. The author and publisher disclaim any liability for any physical, emotional, or psychological consequences that may result from reading this work.

By purchasing and reading this book, you acknowledge that you have read, understood, and agreed to this disclaimer.

Thank you for your understanding and support.

Get A Free Book At: https://free.copypeople.com

---

1. https://copypeople.com/
2. https://copypeople.com/
3. https://free.copypeople.com

Silent Control

Ella's world had always been small, but it had once been enough. She worked as a paralegal, spent her weekends with friends, and saw her family on holidays. There were moments of happiness, flashes of clarity, when she felt like she had a place in the world, even if that place was sometimes blurry and imperfect. But all of that changed when she met Valerie.

Valerie was everything Ella wasn't. Tall, confident, magnetic. She seemed to glide through life, leaving an invisible trail of allure behind her. When they first met, it was at a mutual friend's party. Valerie spoke to Ella with the kind of intensity that made her feel special. She listened when Ella talked, really listened, unlike most people who just nodded along until it was their turn to speak.

Valerie's compliments were so precise, so cuttingly direct, that they peeled away the layers Ella had worked hard to keep intact. "You're so beautiful when you smile," Valerie had said one evening as they sat alone on Ella's couch, the television forgotten between them. "It's a shame you don't let yourself smile more often."

Ella hadn't understood what Valerie meant at the time, but it felt too good to question. Slowly, her relationship with Valerie grew, and with it, a quiet dependency. It wasn't overt at first—just small things, casual remarks that made Ella doubt her own choices. Valerie didn't like Ella's best friend, Claire. "She's too needy, Ella. You don't need that kind of energy in your life," Valerie would say, and Ella, always the one to placate, would nod and agree, pushing Claire's texts to the side. Slowly, Claire faded from Ella's life.

Then there were the comments about her appearance. "You should wear your hair down more. It makes your face look less... angular." Ella had short hair at the time, a pixie cut that she loved. But when Valerie said it, it was different—it felt like a critique wrapped in affection, and so she changed it.

The more she changed, the more Valerie seemed to find fault with her. "Why are you so tense all the time? Relax, Ella. You're so much more attractive when you're at ease."

Valerie taught her to control her body, to smile in the right moments, to hold her posture just so. At first, it was flattering, the idea that someone cared enough to mold her. But with every passing day, Ella lost more of herself. She stopped talking to her coworkers after Valerie pointed out how they made her feel "small" and "irrelevant." She stopped going to the gym after Valerie suggested it might be better for her to "focus on other things," like spending more time with her. The gym became a symbol of everything Ella had to sacrifice for love.

And yet, each time she acquiesced, Valerie rewarded her with attention—affection that felt like validation. It was intoxicating. When Ella hesitated, Valerie would grow distant, cool, and Ella would panic, rushing to fix whatever had gone wrong. She never questioned why she felt that constant knot of anxiety in her stomach. She never wondered why her phone seemed to buzz more frequently with Valerie's messages demanding where she was, who she was with, and why she hadn't checked in for hours.

As weeks became months, Ella began to lose touch with her own reality. Friends she'd once called family became distant memories. Her apartment felt smaller, suffocating, a reflection of her life with Valerie. The world outside their little bubble seemed like a strange, unfamiliar place—one she no longer belonged to.

One evening, Ella stood in front of the mirror, brushing her hair. Her reflection seemed foreign to her, the face looking back not quite matching the person she felt herself to be. The person she thought she had been.

The doorbell rang, and when Valerie entered, her eyes immediately swept over Ella, as if searching for something wrong. "You've been quiet today. You didn't answer my texts."

Ella swallowed. "I was just... thinking."

Valerie leaned against the doorframe, her lips curling into a smirk. "Thinking? About what? If you ever stopped thinking so much, maybe you'd be able to enjoy life more."

Ella's stomach turned. The voice inside her head screamed at her—this wasn't how things were supposed to be. But she couldn't shake it. Valerie was everything now. Without her, there was no air to breathe.

That night, Valerie told Ella that they needed a "fresh start." She suggested that they take a trip together, to clear their heads. "You've been so stressed, babe. Let's go away. Just the two of us."

Ella's pulse quickened at the idea. But she hesitated for only a moment before the familiar fear crept in—the fear of losing Valerie, of not being enough. She nodded, a smile forced onto her lips.

They booked a cabin in the mountains, secluded, quiet. Just as Valerie promised, the cabin was beautiful, but the cold air outside seemed to seep into Ella's soul. She felt like an outsider in the life she'd created. For the first time, she questioned the role she was playing. The next morning, Valerie left to buy groceries, leaving Ella alone. And in that stillness, Ella's mind raced. She reached for her phone, scanning through her old messages, pictures of Claire, of her family. She had a life once, before Valerie.

When Valerie returned, Ella didn't hide her confusion. "Val," she began slowly, her voice shaking, "I... I don't know if this is working anymore. I feel like I've lost myself."

Valerie's face hardened, and she closed the door with a force that echoed in the empty room. "Lost yourself?" she said, her voice cold now, no longer warm and familiar. "No, Ella. You never had a self to begin with. You were just a blank canvas, and I made you beautiful."

Ella recoiled. For the first time, the scales fell from her eyes. All the smiles, the tenderness—was it ever real? Or was it just a methodical, cruel manipulation?

Valerie stepped closer, her gaze sharp, like a predator closing in on prey. "You were nothing before me. Just a sad little girl who needed me. I gave you purpose. And now, you're nothing again."

Ella's breath hitched as the gravity of Valerie's words sank in. Her sense of self, the small fragments she had tried to rebuild, felt as though they were being stripped away, one by one. And then, in the silence that followed, she realized something terrifying: Valerie's power had never been about love. It had been about control, about shaping and reshaping Ella into something she could own. It wasn't affection that had bound her, but fear.

Ella backed away, stumbling toward the door. "I'm leaving. I'm done."

Valerie watched her, a slight, almost imperceptible smile curling at the corner of her lips. "You can leave, but you'll never be free, Ella. I'll always be inside your head."

The door slammed behind Ella as she stepped out into the night, but she knew the truth now. Valerie had never just loved her. She had never wanted Ella to be herself—only what Valerie needed her to be.

And as the dark road stretched out before her, Ella understood, with a clarity that was both painful and freeing, that real freedom came not in leaving, but in reclaiming the parts of herself that had once seemed so easy to give away.

Gaslighted

Hannah had always been a bit forgetful. At least, that's what Emily said. Emily, with her perfect smile and soft voice, always knew the right way to put things, always knew how to make everything seem like it was just a misunderstanding. It had been easy to fall for Emily, or rather, for the version of herself Emily had crafted for her. She was soft, gentle, caring, with just the right amount of charisma to make Hannah feel like she was special, the only one who could see her true self.

But something had shifted over the past few months. Hannah couldn't quite put her finger on it, but small things had begun to feel off. Emily's compliments, once so sincere, now had a sharpness to them. "You forgot to bring the keys again, Hannah," she'd say with a tight smile, her voice dripping with frustration. "How can you be so careless?"

It had been a long day at work, and Hannah was tired. Her mind wasn't firing on all cylinders. "I'm sorry, Em. I'll get them tomorrow."

But Emily had shaken her head. "No, you won't. You always say that, but you don't. You never do what you say you'll do."

Hannah wanted to protest, wanted to defend herself, but something inside her hesitated. Maybe it was the tone in Emily's voice or the flicker of judgment in her eyes. It was as if she were being stripped bare of all the goodness she had believed she possessed. So, instead of arguing, she retreated inward, swallowing the guilt and letting it turn sour in her stomach.

Over the next few weeks, more moments like this crept in. Emily would casually mention things Hannah had supposedly done or said, but Hannah couldn't remember. The vague sense of unease kept growing, gnawing at her, but Emily was so good at making her feel like she was the one at fault, like she was just overreacting. "You're too sensitive, Hannah. Honestly. It's just a simple mistake. Why are you always making everything a bigger deal than it is?"

It wasn't that Emily was overtly cruel. It was the way she twisted the knife with such subtlety, such finesse, that it left Hannah unsure whether she was imagining it. "Didn't you say we were going to the restaurant last night?" Emily asked one evening, eyes narrowing as she put away her keys.

Hannah was sure she had told Emily, but the way Emily was looking at her made her question it. "No, I didn't. I—I thought I said we weren't going tonight."

"Really?" Emily's voice was light, mocking. "Because I distinctly remember you telling me we were going, and you were all excited about it."

"No. I—" Hannah faltered. Was she losing her mind? She had been so sure. "I don't think I did."

Emily's lips curled into a smile, but it wasn't a kind one. "You know, it's really exhausting when you can't even remember what you said five minutes ago. It's like I'm living with a stranger."

Hannah's pulse quickened, the familiar feeling of unease creeping into her chest. She hated this feeling—this sense of being slowly undone, piece by piece. Every time she tried to stand up for herself, Emily would counter with a soft-spoken rebuttal, expertly undermining her confidence. She began to dread coming home. She started second-guessing herself. Had she really said that thing? Had she really forgotten something? The voice in her head became louder, more insistent.

"You've been acting distant lately, Hannah," Emily would say as they sat on the couch together, her hand resting on Hannah's leg. "I don't know what's going on with you, but I'm trying, I really am. Can't you just appreciate that?"

Hannah wanted to scream, to tell Emily that it wasn't her—*she* was the one who was changing. But every time she tried, she would see that hurt expression on Emily's face, and her own doubt would creep in. "Maybe I am being distant. Maybe I've been too harsh."

There was no real anger in Emily's voice, just disappointment. The kind that made Hannah want to crumble. "I'm just trying to make things work, but you're so closed off sometimes. I just don't understand why you keep pushing me away."

The next day, Hannah caught herself staring at her phone, hesitating before sending a message to a friend. She couldn't remember the last time she had talked to anyone about anything real. She couldn't remember the last time she'd laughed in earnest, or shared something with someone who wasn't Emily. The isolation was subtle, but it was there, like a dark thread weaving through her life. She wasn't sure if she could trust her own mind anymore.

One night, after another argument about forgotten plans, Hannah went into the kitchen to get a glass of water. She was shaking, her stomach churning. It felt like her brain was fogged, like she was walking through a dream. As she filled the glass, she caught a glimpse of herself in the reflection of the microwave door—her eyes were red and puffy, her face pale, like she hadn't slept in days. She hadn't, really. Not properly. And the worst part was that she didn't even know how long this had been going on.

Suddenly, she heard Emily behind her. "You're still doing this, huh? Are you *really* going to pretend that you didn't forget the meeting this morning?"

Hannah turned, startled. "I—I didn't forget the meeting. I—"

But Emily was already shaking her head. "You did. You don't even remember it, do you?" She smiled sweetly, but the cruelty behind her eyes was unmistakable. "I can't keep doing this with you, Hannah. It's exhausting."

Hannah stood frozen, her heart pounding in her chest. The words were too much, too much for her to handle. "I don't—"

"Of course you don't," Emily interrupted, her voice now soft but biting. "You can't even remember simple things. And that's *my* fault?"

For the first time, Hannah felt a cold clarity surge through her. She was suffocating in this relationship, buried under the weight of her own self-doubt. Emily had trained her to doubt her every instinct, every thought, until she had no idea what was real anymore. But standing there, with Emily's voice still ringing in her ears, something inside Hannah snapped.

"I'm not crazy," she whispered, almost to herself, as she backed away from Emily, the words falling from her lips like a lifeline. "You're making me crazy."

Emily's eyes flashed, but it wasn't fear. It was something else—a sick satisfaction. "You really think I've been doing that, Hannah?" She chuckled, but it wasn't a laugh; it was something darker, something predatory. "Sweetheart, you were crazy long before I came along. You just didn't know it."

And in that moment, as Emily's smile twisted into something dangerous, Hannah realized the truth—she had never been the one losing her mind. It had always been Emily, twisting the world around her until nothing was real. And now, as she stood there, her mind suddenly clear for the first time in so long, she knew what she had to do.

But it was already too late. Emily had already won.

The Financial Trap

Lucy had always been independent. She prided herself on her job, her apartment, her freedom. She had worked her way up in her career, taking pride in the small victories: the promotion, the raise, the ability to pay her own rent without any help from anyone. But that was before she met Erica.

Erica was charming, magnetic, and warm in a way that made Lucy feel seen. It was easy to fall for her. They met at a party thrown by a mutual friend, and there was something intoxicating about Erica's confidence. She had a way of making people feel like they were the most important person in the room, as if their every word mattered.

In the beginning, everything felt effortless. Erica would text her throughout the day, always checking in, always making sure Lucy felt supported. "I love how driven you are, Luce," she would say. "But you know, you work so hard. You deserve a break." Lucy would laugh it off, telling Erica that her work was a source of pride. But Erica would counter, her voice soft yet persuasive. "You deserve to enjoy life too, you know? Why don't you let me take care of things for a while?"

At first, Lucy shrugged it off as a sweet suggestion, not thinking too much about it. But then, over time, Erica's comments started to sink in. "You're so smart, so talented, you could do so much more if you didn't have to work all the time." Her voice was laced with affection, but there was an undercurrent of something else. Something that Lucy couldn't quite place at the time.

When Erica suggested that Lucy quit her job and focus on "what really mattered"—their relationship—Lucy was hesitant. "You know, I've worked so hard to get where I am. I can't just leave it all behind."

Erica had laughed softly, caressing her cheek. "You don't have to leave everything behind, babe. Just give yourself some time off. You'll feel so much better, I promise. I can support us for a while, and you can just relax. You deserve to be happy."

It was that word—"deserve"—that kept echoing in Lucy's mind. Erica's words painted a picture of a life where Lucy didn't have to worry about work, about finances, about stress. She could just be, with Erica. And what harm could there be in trying it for a while? After all, Erica was more than capable of handling things. She was successful, well-off, and she seemed to genuinely care about Lucy's well-being.

So, Lucy quit her job.

At first, it was blissful. The days were spent lounging in bed, cooking meals together, watching movies, and going on long walks. Erica's business was thriving, and Lucy didn't have to worry about a thing. "You look so much happier, Luce," Erica would say with a smile, pressing a kiss to the top of her head. "You deserve this."

But as the weeks turned into months, things began to change. Erica would ask for small favors, little things that Lucy didn't mind doing at first—running errands, picking up groceries, or helping with the house. But soon, those requests became more frequent. "Can you just take care of this bill? I'm too busy with work," Erica would say, her voice light, as though it was no trouble at all. And Lucy, feeling the weight of her financial dependence, complied.

Soon, it wasn't just about the bills. Erica began dictating how Lucy spent her days. "You really don't need to buy anything unnecessary, Luce. Let's focus on saving. I've been thinking we should get rid of your credit cards. Just use the ones I have—much simpler that way, don't you think?"

Lucy hesitated, but Erica's reasoning made sense. "I'm taking care of everything, Luce. You don't need to worry about the small stuff."

It felt nice at first, that sense of security, knowing Erica was in control. But slowly, the control shifted, subtly and without warning. Erica began to dictate Lucy's every purchase, even the smallest ones. "I think we should buy a new couch, don't you? You don't need that old thing anymore." Lucy had no say in it—Erica simply bought the new one and had it delivered while Lucy was out.

As the months passed, Erica started to push boundaries even further. "I know you want to keep that old dress, but it's so outdated. You don't need it anymore. I'll take care of it for you." It wasn't about the dress. It wasn't about the couch. It was about Lucy's sense of autonomy, slowly being chipped away. Erica would make decisions without asking, buying things Lucy didn't need, rearranging her schedule, telling her when to be ready, when to go out, when to rest.

One evening, Lucy found herself standing in front of the mirror, staring at the woman she no longer recognized. Her hair was unkempt, her clothes loose and worn, a shadow of who she once was. She couldn't remember the last time she'd made a decision for herself, the last time she had chosen something simply because it made her happy.

She picked up her phone, scrolling through her contacts. But when she saw her friends' names, her stomach churned with unease. She hadn't spoken to them in months. Not since Erica had started making subtle comments about "toxic" people and "bad influences." "Your friends just don't understand you, Luce," Erica would say. "They'll pull you back into that old, stressful life. We don't need them. We have each other."

Lucy had pushed her friends away. She had distanced herself from family. Erica had made it all seem like it was for her own good, for her happiness. But now, standing in the dim light of the apartment, the weight of her isolation pressed down on her chest.

Erica entered the room, her face soft, her smile kind. "What's wrong, baby?" she asked, slipping behind Lucy and wrapping her arms around her waist.

"I... I think I want to start working again," Lucy said quietly, the words tasting foreign on her tongue.

Erica's smile faltered, just for a moment. "Don't be silly. You're better off without the stress. I'll take care of everything. We're a team, remember?"

Lucy's heart raced, her pulse quickening with a sense of unease. But the truth had already begun to settle within her. She wasn't part of a team. She was a cog in Erica's machine, a pawn in a game she didn't even know she was playing.

And in that moment, Lucy realized something terrifying: she wasn't just financially dependent. She was emotionally, psychologically dependent, too. Erica had trapped her in a gilded cage, convincing her that this life, this suffocating control, was love.

Lucy's hand shook as she reached for the door. But Erica's voice followed her, calm and soothing. "Where are you going, Luce? We're meant to be together."

Lucy paused, the weight of her decision pressing on her. She could leave, could fight back, but the fear, the doubt, the years of being molded, kept her frozen. As Erica's arms encircled her waist once more, Lucy couldn't help but feel the heavy chains of the life she had chosen.

She had traded freedom for comfort, and now it was too late. There was no going back.

Bleeding Heart

Abigail's life had always been a balancing act. She was a caretaker by nature, a woman who thrived on giving—whether it was to her job, her family, or her relationships. But there was one person who had always required more of her than she could give. Maya.

Maya had appeared in Abigail's life like a storm, sudden and intense. She was everything Abigail wasn't: chaotic, unpredictable, and magnetic. Maya's sadness seemed so deep, so profound, that Abigail couldn't help but want to fix it. She wanted to be the one to make things better, to be the one person who could bring her peace. It was this desire to heal that kept Abigail tethered to Maya, despite everything else.

In the beginning, their relationship was full of passion and intensity, the kind of love that swallows you whole. Maya would speak to Abigail in whispered confessions, her voice thick with tears and vulnerability. "I don't know what I'd do without you," she'd say, her hands trembling as she touched Abigail's arm. "You're the only one who understands me. If you ever left... I don't think I could survive."

Abigail would hold her, tell her it was okay, that she'd never leave. She believed her own words. The need to be needed was so consuming, so entwined with her own identity, that she couldn't imagine anything else. She believed that she had found someone who truly relied on her, someone who saw her as essential, irreplaceable.

But soon, the subtle signs of manipulation began to creep in. Maya would call Abigail constantly, interrupting her work, demanding her attention. "Where are you? Why haven't you texted me back? Don't you care about me anymore?" Her voice was always small, hurt, as though Abigail's failure to immediately respond was a betrayal. Abigail would drop everything, rush to Maya's side, and fix whatever had gone wrong, believing that it was her responsibility to make everything okay.

As time went on, the demands became more desperate, more frequent. It started with small things—Maya insisting that Abigail stay the night, even when she had early meetings the next day. "I need you here. Don't leave me alone tonight," she'd say, and Abigail, unable to say no, would stay. But the requests soon escalated. "I'm not feeling well," Maya would text, and even if it was just a bad mood or a minor headache, Abigail would rush over, her heart heavy with the weight of the need to be there.

One night, when Abigail had stayed later than usual, Maya suddenly pulled away. She sat on the couch, arms folded, her face unreadable. "Why do you always leave me, Abigail? Why does everyone leave me?" Maya's voice was barely above a whisper.

Abigail felt her chest tighten. "Maya, no one's leaving you. I'm here. I'm not going anywhere."

But Maya shook her head slowly, tears welling in her eyes. "If you leave me, I'll hurt myself. I can't do this without you. I can't handle it. I'll just—" She stopped herself, her body trembling, as if the mere thought of abandonment was too much to bear.

The words hung in the air like a blade, sharp and cold. Abigail felt her heart break, a visceral ache that sank deep. "Don't say that, Maya," she whispered. "Please. I'm not going anywhere. I promise. I'm not leaving."

Maya met her eyes, her lips curling into a faint, almost imperceptible smile. "You're sure?" she asked, the vulnerability in her voice laced with something darker, something more manipulative.

Abigail nodded quickly, the promise slipping from her lips before she even realized the cost of it. "I'm not leaving you. You mean too much to me."

But it wasn't enough. As the days passed, the cycle continued. Maya would call, text, demand more. Her depression deepened, her self-harm became more frequent, and every time, Abigail found herself trapped deeper in the web of guilt that Maya wove around her.

Abigail began to lose track of time, of who she was. She gave up dinners with friends, canceled plans with family, ignored her own needs. Every day, every minute, she was focused solely on Maya. There was nothing else. If she wasn't at Maya's side, she was consumed by worry, wondering if Maya was okay, wondering if she would be there when she got back.

One evening, Abigail returned to Maya's apartment after yet another missed dinner with her parents. Maya was sitting on the couch, her face buried in her hands. "You were gone for so long," Maya whispered, her voice barely audible. "I thought you didn't love me anymore."

Abigail dropped her bag by the door, guilt rising in her throat. "Maya, I—"

"I need you to promise me something," Maya interrupted, her eyes glassy. "Promise me you'll always stay with me. That no matter what, you'll never leave. I can't do this without you, Abigail. I can't breathe without you."

Abigail could feel her own sense of self slipping away, the weight of Maya's words pressing her into the ground. "I'm here, Maya. I'm not going anywhere."

"Promise me," Maya repeated, her eyes wide, searching for validation.

"I promise," Abigail said, her voice hollow.

The following week, things escalated further. Maya's behavior became erratic, her mood swings more violent. One moment she was sweet, desperate for Abigail's attention, and the next she was angry, accusing Abigail of not caring enough, of abandoning her. Each time Abigail tried to pull away for a moment of personal space, Maya would threaten to hurt herself, to fall apart. "You're all I have," she'd sob, her voice breaking. "If you leave me, I'll die. You know that, right? You're the only reason I'm still here."

Abigail's own life had become a series of apologies, of justifications, of promises to stay, to never leave. She had forgotten what it was like to be her own person, to do things without fear of the consequences. The person she had once been was slipping away, replaced by a constant, oppressive need to fulfill Maya's demands.

One night, as Abigail sat on the couch, staring blankly at the TV, her phone buzzed with a message from Maya. "I can't do this anymore. I'm sorry, I've messed everything up. I'm just too broken."

Abigail's heart clenched. She had seen this before. The threats. The words of despair. The manipulation. She stood up, pacing, her hands shaking. *What if this time it was real?* she thought. *What if I'm too late?*

Without thinking, Abigail rushed to Maya's apartment, her pulse quickening with fear. When she arrived, the door was slightly ajar. She pushed it open, calling Maya's name softly.

There, on the floor, was Maya. But she wasn't lying lifeless. She wasn't even hurt.

Maya looked up at Abigail, her eyes glistening with an unreadable expression. "You came," she said quietly, almost too calmly.

Abigail froze, her breath catching in her throat. "What are you doing? You scared me. You said..."

Maya stood up, brushing her hair from her face. "You always come when I need you," she said, smiling darkly. "I knew you would. I just wanted to make sure you'd never leave. I knew I could get you to stay."

Abigail felt the floor fall out beneath her. She had given up everything, her life, her identity, just to satisfy a need that was never real. Maya had never intended to leave. She had never needed her. Abigail had only been another way to feed her own control.

In that moment, Abigail realized the truth: Maya had never loved her. She had only loved the power of keeping her trapped. And now, standing in the cold, silent room, Abigail could finally see that the only person she needed to save was herself.

But the door had already closed behind her, and the darkness of that realization began to bleed into everything else.

This content may violate our usage policies[1].

Did we get it wrong? Please tell us by giving this response a thumbs down.

---

[1] https://openai.com/policies/usage-policies

The Perfect Life

Sophie had never been one for grand gestures. She liked simple things—a quiet walk in the park, a cup of coffee in the morning, the sound of rain against the window. But when she met Olivia, everything seemed to shift. Olivia was different from anyone Sophie had ever known—confident, bold, with a kind of magnetic presence that drew people in. Sophie, who had always been more reserved, found herself swept up in Olivia's energy, her laughter, and the way she made Sophie feel special, seen in a way that no one had before.

In the beginning, it felt like a whirlwind romance, fast and intense, each day more exciting than the last. Olivia seemed to have everything figured out. She was successful, charming, and had a network of friends and colleagues who adored her. Sophie felt like she was finally part of something larger than herself. Olivia was the center of that world, and Sophie was content to orbit around her, basking in the warmth of her attention.

But as the months passed, Sophie started to notice subtle changes. Olivia began to subtly steer her away from the people she'd once been closest to—her family, her friends. "You don't need them, Soph," Olivia would say, her voice soft, but persuasive. "We have everything we need right here. Why do you need to go see your sister again? She's just going to ask about your job and make you feel bad about it."

At first, Sophie brushed it off. She loved Olivia, and maybe Olivia just wanted to protect her from the things that caused her stress. After all, Olivia always had her best interests at heart. But slowly, the distance between Sophie and her old life began to grow. The visits with her family became less frequent. Her friends, who once called and texted regularly, were met with Sophie's increasingly vague responses. Olivia didn't demand Sophie cut ties with anyone, but she made it clear that time spent with others was time taken away from their "perfect" life together.

Olivia would make little comments that seemed harmless at first. "I just don't understand why your friends don't get it. Why can't they see how great we are together? It's like they're trying to pull you away from me." Sophie, in turn, found herself defending Olivia, explaining that her friends didn't understand, that they were just concerned because Sophie had always been the quiet one, the one who needed more time to adjust.

Gradually, Olivia's influence over Sophie grew stronger. She started taking more control over Sophie's daily life. The places they went, the things they did, all became choices Olivia made for both of them. Sophie's small acts of rebellion—going for a run without Olivia, sending a message to a friend she hadn't heard from in weeks—were met with sharp disapproval. "Why would you want to do that without me? Do you know how hurtful that is?" Olivia's voice was calm, but Sophie could hear the strain beneath it.

Sophie tried to explain that she just needed some space, but Olivia would always turn it around, making Sophie feel selfish, making her feel like she was doing something wrong by wanting a few moments of solitude. "You don't need to go to yoga, Soph. It's just a distraction. You have me, and I am all you'll ever need."

And Sophie believed her. Slowly, insidiously, the outside world began to feel less important. Olivia had made everything so perfect, so serene. They cooked together, traveled together, spent every waking moment together. And Sophie, in her quiet desperation to make Olivia happy, to preserve the delicate balance of their life, gave in. She stopped seeing her family, stopped reaching out to her friends. She stopped thinking about the life she had before Olivia. After all, Olivia was right—she had everything she needed.

Then, one night, Sophie received a message from her best friend, Chloe. It had been months since they'd last talked. Chloe had reached out, asking Sophie if she was okay, if she was still coming to the annual holiday dinner at her parents' house. Sophie stared at the message for a long moment, her heart pounding. She hadn't told Olivia about Chloe's message, hadn't mentioned the dinner in weeks. Olivia had always been critical of the things Chloe said, the way she questioned their relationship.

Sophie put the phone down quickly, her mind spinning. She knew what would happen if she mentioned it. Olivia would be disappointed, and Sophie couldn't bear the thought of losing her. Olivia had always made her feel like everything was fine, that their life together was perfect. The thought of stepping outside that bubble—of reintroducing anything from the old life—felt overwhelming.

Sophie ignored the message, deleting it without a second thought. She would tell Chloe that she was too busy, too wrapped up in the "perfect" life Olivia had created for them. After all, she didn't need anyone else. She had Olivia.

Days passed, and Olivia noticed the change in Sophie. Sophie had been quieter, more withdrawn, and Olivia, ever the perceptive one, asked what was wrong. Sophie explained that she had just been feeling a bit off, but Olivia wasn't satisfied. "You're not telling me everything, Sophie. You know you can tell me anything, don't you?" Her voice was gentle, but Sophie could hear the unspoken demand beneath it.

Sophie took a deep breath. She couldn't keep this from Olivia. She had to confess that she had heard from Chloe, that she had ignored her message. But the words felt stuck in her throat. Olivia's eyes darkened as Sophie spoke. "Chloe, huh?" she said, her voice sharp. "You should've told me. You should have asked me if it was okay to talk to her. You should have known that I don't like her."

Sophie recoiled slightly, the weight of the words hitting her harder than she expected. "I—I didn't think it would be a big deal. I just wanted to keep things simple."

"Simple," Olivia repeated, her smile cold and brittle. "That's exactly it, Sophie. You've been so wrapped up in this idea of a 'perfect' life that you've forgotten what really matters. You've forgotten *me*."

Sophie's heart sank. She had known, on some level, that things weren't right. But this—this was different. Olivia wasn't just angry. She was cold. Sophie felt the walls closing in around her, the room shrinking, as if she were suffocating. Olivia stepped closer, her fingers brushing Sophie's cheek. "I've given you everything, Sophie. And you... you go behind my back and talk to people who will just try to ruin what we have. I won't let them, Sophie. I won't let you go back to that life."

Sophie felt the tears welling up in her eyes. She wanted to leave, to run, to find her family, her friends—but she couldn't. Olivia had made it clear. The life Sophie had before, the one that felt like home, was now a distant memory. Olivia had constructed a life so perfect that it had become a prison. And Sophie had walked right into it, willingly, thinking it was freedom.

But there was no way out now. Not for Sophie. Olivia's grip was too strong. The illusion of love had trapped her in a world where there was no escape. The perfect life wasn't real. It was just a trap. And now, Sophie was its prisoner, and she was trapped in the silence of a life she couldn't leave.

A Perfect Lie

Jessie had always been told that relationships were about trust, transparency, and communication. She had grown up on the idea that a successful relationship required honesty, that it was the foundation of any bond worth keeping. And for a time, she believed it. Until she met Clara.

Clara was everything Jessie had ever wanted in a partner—smart, funny, compassionate, and absolutely devoted to her. They had met at a mutual friend's dinner party, and Jessie had been instantly captivated. There was something about Clara's effortless charm, her ability to listen, her willingness to engage that made Jessie feel important, seen. Clara made her feel like she was the only one in the room.

In the beginning, their relationship was everything Jessie had dreamed of. They spent weekends together, sharing long walks and dinners, talking about everything from politics to their childhoods. Clara was always supportive, always present. Jessie couldn't help but fall deeper and deeper into the illusion of love Clara had created. She was the perfect partner, the kind of woman Jessie had imagined when she thought of true love.

But as time passed, Jessie started noticing small things. At first, they were insignificant: an odd text message that Clara quickly dismissed, a phone call that Clara took in another room. But Jessie didn't question it. She trusted Clara completely. And yet, a nagging feeling began to grow in her chest.

One evening, Jessie was curled up on the couch, flipping through a book, when Clara's phone buzzed across the coffee table. Jessie glanced at the screen—an unfamiliar name. *Natalie*. Clara's tone on the phone had been calm but strained when she excused herself to take the call. Jessie didn't think much of it at first, but the seed had been planted.

The days that followed were marked by subtle changes. Clara's affection seemed more distant, her words more clipped. Jessie chalked it up to work stress, or perhaps her own insecurities creeping in. After all, Clara had been nothing but loving for the first year of their relationship. There had to be a rational explanation.

But the late-night texts and whispered phone calls continued. The excuses started to pile up: *It's just a friend I've known for years, Jessie, I'm just helping her with something personal, I'm busy tonight, but I'll make it up to you tomorrow.*

The words felt hollow, and Jessie's doubts began to grow. But still, Clara's warmth, her affection when they were together, was enough to quiet the voice in Jessie's head. It was clear to Jessie that she had become too emotionally invested, too dependent on Clara's validation to question the subtle signs of manipulation.

Then one evening, it all came to a head. Jessie had planned a surprise date for Clara—her favorite restaurant, a bottle of wine, candles. She had been looking forward to the evening, hoping to reconnect after weeks of feeling like she was walking on eggshells. When Clara arrived, she seemed distracted, her phone buzzing incessantly in her pocket. Jessie smiled and greeted her, but Clara's eyes didn't quite meet hers.

"I'm so glad we're doing this," Jessie said, trying to keep the mood light, her heart pounding in her chest.

"Yeah," Clara replied, barely looking up from her phone. "I really needed to get out of the house."

Jessie's stomach twisted, but she forced a smile. "You're okay, right?"

Clara nodded quickly, distracted. "Yeah, just a lot going on at work. But I'm here now, and that's what matters."

As the evening wore on, Jessie couldn't shake the feeling that something was wrong. Clara wasn't engaging with her the way she used to. She wasn't making eye contact, wasn't laughing at Jessie's jokes the way she used to. The words felt forced, hollow. Jessie's mind raced with the possibility that Clara was no longer interested in her, that something had shifted.

After dinner, as they walked out into the cool night air, Jessie couldn't hold it in anymore. "Clara," she began, her voice trembling, "what's going on? You've been so distant lately, and I don't know what I'm doing wrong. I feel like I'm losing you."

Clara stopped walking and turned to face her, her expression unreadable. For a moment, Jessie thought she saw a flicker of guilt in Clara's eyes, but it was gone in an instant. Clara stepped closer, cupping Jessie's face in her hands. "You're not losing me," she said softly, her voice soothing. "You're just overreacting. I've been dealing with a lot, but it has nothing to do with you."

Jessie's chest tightened. "But... but you've been acting so distant. You've been avoiding me. I don't understand."

Clara's eyes softened, but the warmth didn't reach her voice. "It's not you, Jessie. It's me. I've been trying to figure things out, and it's hard when I feel like you're always putting so much pressure on me. I need space."

Jessie's heart sank, the words cutting through her like ice. "What do you mean, space? I'm just trying to connect with you."

Clara sighed, rolling her eyes in a way that made Jessie feel small. "God, you're exhausting sometimes. You never stop to think about how much I'm doing for you. All you ever do is take, take, take. It's draining, and I need to breathe. I need to be able to have my own space without feeling like you're trying to control everything."

Jessie stood there, frozen, feeling the weight of Clara's words press down on her. She had never asked for control, never asked for anything other than to be loved. "I just want to understand," she whispered, her voice barely a breath.

Clara looked away, her expression hardened. "Maybe it's just easier for me to be with someone who doesn't need so much all the time. I don't know if I can give you everything you want anymore."

Jessie stood there, devastated, trying to comprehend what had just been said. "What are you talking about?" she asked, her voice shaking.

Clara's face softened with a mock sympathy. "I think you need to take a step back and look at yourself. Maybe *you* are the problem, Jessie. Maybe you're too much for me to handle. But I'm doing the best I can."

The words hit Jessie like a slap. Clara was twisting the narrative, manipulating her into thinking that it was her fault—that she was the one who was demanding, the one who was too needy.

Jessie's mind raced. It hit her all at once—Clara had been maintaining a double life. She had been keeping Jessie in the dark while emotionally connecting with someone else, someone who wasn't so demanding, so needy. Clara wasn't pulling away because of work stress or personal issues. She was pulling away because Jessie had become a burden, an obstacle in the way of her emotional affairs.

And in that moment, Jessie understood. Clara wasn't the one who needed space. It was Jessie who needed to escape.

But the realization came too late. Jessie had already been trapped in the web of Clara's manipulation, and the perfect lie had become her prison.

The Cost of Saving Her

Maggie was a woman of charm and subtlety. At least, that's how she made herself seem. She'd built a life around the art of being needed, perfecting the skill of drawing sympathy and attention from those around her. But it wasn't her fault. Maggie wasn't a bad person. She wasn't malicious. She was just... broken, or so she told herself, or so she told everyone else. Her life, she would say, had been a series of disasters. She'd lost her family, her career had fallen apart, her friends had betrayed her. She was the perpetual victim, and anyone who saw her with the right eyes could not help but feel the overwhelming urge to "save" her.

That's how she met Kyle. She was sitting alone at a café when he noticed her. There was something about her, the way she tucked her hair behind her ear, the sadness in her eyes that seemed too heavy for her slender frame. He struck up a conversation, and it didn't take long before she began telling him her story—the abandonment, the struggles, the chaos she had endured. She wasn't looking for sympathy, she said, just understanding.

Kyle, always the empath, could hardly resist. He found himself drawn into her world, eager to help, to fix whatever had gone wrong in her life. She didn't ask for much. Just time, just company, just someone to listen. Over time, he started feeling like her personal knight in shining armor.

Her world, full of broken promises and bad memories, was the kind of place Kyle knew he could make better. He could be her hero. She would whisper these words to him at night, when their bodies tangled together. "You're the only one who really sees me, Kyle. You're the only one who understands."

It wasn't long before Maggie's problems escalated. The floodgates opened, and suddenly, every day was a crisis. Her job was always on the line, her landlord was threatening eviction, and her health—oh, her health—was always teetering on the edge of disaster. Kyle would rush to her side, no matter what. Late nights spent fixing things, reassuring her that everything would be okay. And every time, Maggie's gratitude was overwhelming. "I don't know what I'd do without you, Kyle. You're my savior."

Kyle loved the feeling. The feeling of being needed, of being indispensable. Every time she fell apart, he swooped in, fixing her life piece by piece. Slowly, he began to lose track of his own needs, his own desires. He neglected his friends, his career ambitions, his hobbies. Maggie's crises became his crises. He told himself it was worth it. That this was love.

At first, Kyle tried to balance it all—his career, his responsibilities, and Maggie's ever-growing need for attention. But eventually, it became impossible. Maggie's calls would come at the most inconvenient times, her tears would fall during meetings or while he was out with friends. And every time, he would drop everything for her. She had a way of making him feel like the only thing that mattered in the world was making her life manageable. If he could just make her happy, if he could just keep fixing things, then everything would be okay.

Maggie was a master at making Kyle feel like her knight in shining armor. She'd tell him that without him, she would fall apart. "You saved me from myself, Kyle," she'd say, her voice full of vulnerability. "I couldn't survive without you. You're my everything."

The words became like a drug. Kyle felt his sense of purpose tied to her brokenness, his identity wrapped up in her suffering. But over time, the cracks in the façade began to show. Maggie's tears weren't always real. Her crises weren't always urgent. And sometimes, the things she claimed were broken—her job, her relationships, her health—seemed to be remarkably convenient for her to talk about, but not as urgent as she made them seem.

Kyle's friends started noticing. They told him he was losing himself. "You've changed," they'd say. "You don't even hang out with us anymore. You're always with her." But Maggie would manipulate him into guilt. "If you loved me, you'd be here. If you loved me, you wouldn't abandon me like everyone else."

He didn't realize it at first, but Maggie was slowly taking control of his life. She wasn't just leaning on him for support—she was using him to prop up her existence. And each time Kyle gave in, each time he sacrificed more of his own needs to make sure Maggie was okay, she responded with gratitude, with affection, and with love. But it was always conditional. Her love, her gratitude, came at a price: his time, his attention, his sense of self.

One day, Kyle found himself sitting alone in his apartment, staring at his phone. Maggie had called him again, and this time, her voice was filled with more distress than usual. "Kyle, I don't know how much longer I can keep going like this. I feel so lost, and I don't know if I can handle it anymore. You're all I have, and I need you now more than ever."

Kyle's heart raced. He loved her, of course he loved her. But he couldn't deny the truth that had been creeping into his mind for months now. He was exhausted. He was drowning in her needs, and somewhere along the way, he'd lost the parts of himself that had made him whole. But every time he tried to pull away, Maggie would reel him back in, playing the perfect victim, making him feel like the failure if he couldn't save her.

That night, Kyle sat in the dark, questioning everything. He realized that Maggie wasn't just emotionally dependent on him—she had come to rely on his guilt. She had learned how to manipulate him, how to make him feel like her savior, and she had played that role to perfection. She wasn't just struggling—she was thriving in her victimhood, keeping him tied to her in a way that no amount of love could break.

Maggie's tears had never been about her suffering. They were about control. The control she had over Kyle's life, over his choices, over his identity. And when she sensed him pulling away, when she saw the doubt in his eyes, she knew exactly what to do. She would play the victim again, painting herself as the fragile soul who would fall apart without him.

That night, after a particularly draining phone call, Kyle hung up. He knew what he had to do. He couldn't save her anymore. He couldn't fix everything for her. He had to save himself.

But when he called her the next day to tell her the truth, to finally set boundaries, Maggie's voice cracked. "You don't love me, Kyle. I've given you everything. You said you would always be here for me, and now you're abandoning me. You're just like everyone else."

And in that moment, Kyle realized something horrible. The tears were never real. The victimhood, the constant need, the emotional blackmail—it had all been a game. Maggie didn't need saving. She just needed someone to feed her sense of worth through constant manipulation. And now, as he looked at his phone, he saw the final truth: it wasn't her life he had been fixing all this time. It was his own, which had been destroyed in the process.

And there was no going back.

The Green-Eyed Shadow

It started small, almost innocuously. Emma would glance at Jason's phone when it buzzed, a casual look over his shoulder, her eyes scanning the screen. "Who's Sarah?" she'd ask, her voice light but with just enough of an edge to make him hesitate. Jason would laugh, brushing it off with a nonchalant reply. "Just a coworker. Don't worry about it."

But Emma did worry. Not outwardly, not at first, but deep down, in the quiet spaces of her mind. There was something about Sarah, something that Emma couldn't quite put her finger on. Sarah had a way of laughing, a way of touching Jason's arm just a little too much at work events, too much for Emma's comfort. And every time Emma asked about it, Jason would shrug it off as nothing. "You're overthinking things, Em. She's just a friend."

But Emma knew. She could feel the tension in the air when Sarah's name came up. She could see the little smiles Jason gave when he received a message from her, the spark in his eyes that he didn't even try to hide. He might not have realized it, but Emma could.

One night, as they sat on the couch, Emma couldn't resist anymore. She'd been watching Jason out of the corner of her eye as he scrolled through his phone. The moment felt fragile, like something was on the brink of breaking. "I don't know, Jase. I just feel like you've been a little distant lately. Always on your phone, always busy with work. You barely talk to me anymore."

Jason set his phone down, a slight frown on his face. "That's ridiculous. I'm right here with you. What's going on?"

Emma bit her lip, pretending to be casual, pretending she didn't feel the growing pit in her stomach. "I don't know. Just... sometimes it feels like there's more between you and Sarah than you let on."

Jason's face darkened instantly, his tone shifting, becoming defensive. "What are you talking about? It's nothing. She's just a colleague. You need to trust me more, Em."

But Emma had seen something different. It was the way Sarah's messages lingered, the way Jason always seemed to have an excuse to talk to her, to share things with her that he never shared with Emma. It wasn't just an innocent friendship. She knew it.

As the days passed, Emma's jealousy began to take root. The small doubts festered into bigger ones. Every time Jason was on his phone, every time he smiled at a message, Emma felt a flicker of panic rise in her chest. She started watching him more closely, keeping track of when he left the house, who he talked to, who he spent time with. She began digging into his social media, checking for any traces of Sarah's presence, feeling the weight of insecurity grow heavier with each passing day.

One evening, Emma decided to take things a step further. She planted a seed. At dinner, she casually mentioned Sarah's name again. "You know, Jase, I think Sarah might be interested in you. I mean, I can see the way she looks at you sometimes. She's always texting you, always wanting to be around you."

Jason set down his fork with a sigh, rubbing his temples. "Why are you doing this? You're making something out of nothing. I told you, she's just a colleague. She means nothing to me."

Emma nodded slowly, a small, almost imperceptible smile tugging at the corners of her lips. "I know. I just don't trust her. There's something off about her. I can see it. It's like she wants to take you from me."

Jason's eyes narrowed. "You're being paranoid."

Emma let the words hang in the air, carefully placed. "Am I? I mean, she's always messaging you late at night. Why does she need you at all hours of the day? And when you're not around, she seems to fill that space, doesn't she? Doesn't that make you think, just a little?"

Jason looked away, a flicker of doubt crossing his face. "I don't know. Maybe you're right. Maybe I've been too focused on work."

That small crack in his armor was all Emma needed. From that point on, she manipulated the situation further, stirring the pot with every conversation, every subtle comment. She'd talk about Sarah's flirty behavior, mentioning the way Sarah's eyes lingered on Jason during meetings. She'd talk about how Sarah always seemed to need Jason's help, always leaning on him for things she could do herself. She twisted his doubts, planted them like seeds in his mind, and watched them grow.

As days turned into weeks, Jason's behavior began to change. His confidence wavered. He'd check his phone more frequently, his eyes flicking to Emma nervously when he replied to messages. He started questioning his every move, unsure of what Emma might think. His once easy-going nature became tense, his smiles less frequent. He would come home later and later, excuses flowing easier than truths. Emma, meanwhile, kept pushing the narrative. "You're getting distant. I don't think you even care about me anymore. Maybe it's Sarah. Maybe you've been too caught up in her. I don't know what to believe anymore."

The emotional toll on Jason grew heavier. He felt as though he was walking on eggshells, afraid of making a wrong move, of falling into Emma's trap. His friendships suffered, his family visits became strained. He couldn't bring himself to talk to anyone about the growing fear gnawing at him, because deep down, he wasn't sure if Emma was right. Was he blind to something? Was Sarah a threat to his relationship? Every time he tried to assert himself, to push back against Emma's accusations, the doubts would creep in again, amplified by her words.

One night, after another tense argument over Sarah's "inappropriate" behavior, Jason snapped. He was tired of the constant questioning, the constant sense of being trapped in a web of jealousy and paranoia. "Fine, Emma," he said, his voice shaking with frustration. "Maybe you're right. Maybe I'm too close to Sarah. I'll stop talking to her. I'll end it. But I need you to stop doing this to me."

Emma's eyes glinted with triumph, but she didn't show it. "I just want you to choose me, Jase. I just want you to care enough."

Jason's exhaustion was palpable. He agreed, but his words were empty, resigned. Emma had won. She had forced him into submission.

Weeks passed, and the rift between them deepened. Jason had cut off all contact with Sarah, but it wasn't enough. Emma continued to manipulate him, her hold on him tightening, suffocating. He couldn't escape, not even when he tried.

But as Emma watched Jason's deterioration, a strange realization crept into her mind. She had gotten exactly what she wanted, hadn't she? She had pushed him away from his friends, from his family, from anyone who might have seen what she was doing. And now, Jason was completely hers. But the cost of it all—his happiness, his sanity—was far more than she had anticipated.

And as Jason sank deeper into the hole she had dug for him, Emma couldn't help but wonder: was it worth it? Did she truly need his undivided attention? Or had she created the perfect prison for herself, as well?

In the end, it wasn't just Jason who had been consumed by jealousy. Emma had, too. And now, the only thing left between them was the quiet echo of their broken trust.

The Hollow Comfort

Lena had never seen Jack like this before. He had always been the type of person to brush off hardship with a wry smile or a self-deprecating joke, but now, with his mother's sudden death, he was a shadow of himself. His eyes were dull, as if all the light had been sucked from them. His once steady hands trembled, and his voice, when he spoke, was barely above a whisper. It had been only a week since the funeral, but the grief had already wrapped its claws around him, pulling him into a suffocating spiral.

Lena had always prided herself on being strong, on being the one people turned to when they were in need. And Jack, she knew, needed her. He had always been the one to take care of things—his life was organized, his plans were clear. But now, she was the one who had to take control. She could see how lost he was, how much he struggled to even get out of bed in the mornings, and the idea that he needed someone to help him pick up the pieces felt comforting to her. She could be the one to fix him. To be indispensable.

She had been there for him from the moment the news broke. The day they'd gotten the call about his mother's stroke, Lena had dropped everything. She had been the one to drive him to the hospital, the one to stay by his side as his mother's life slipped away. She had held his hand while he cried, whispered words of comfort that he barely heard. In that moment, she could see how fragile he was, how deeply he loved his mother—and how desperate he was for someone to lean on. She had given him that, become the support he so obviously needed.

But as the days passed and the funeral arrangements were made, Lena found herself doing more than just comforting him. She began making decisions for him. She took charge of the funeral details, choosing the flowers, the music, the guest list. She made sure that his family's house was in order, that the paperwork for his mother's estate was handled, and that he didn't have to worry about anything other than getting through the day. Jack barely noticed, too lost in his grief to care, and Lena felt a growing satisfaction with the control she had over his life.

She could feel the shift inside her, like a door opening. There was something intoxicating about being the one who held the pieces of Jack's life together. As the days turned into weeks, she began to subtly isolate him from his own family and friends. She told him that they would only add to his burden, that it was better for him to focus on healing and that she was all he needed. At first, Jack had hesitated. He had mentioned wanting to talk to his sister, Allison, or maybe going out to dinner with his old college friends, but Lena quickly shot down the idea. "They don't understand, Jack," she would say, her voice sweet but firm. "They're not here. You don't need anyone but me right now. Let me take care of everything."

And so, Jack did what she said. He stopped calling his friends. He barely spoke to his sister. He let Lena make every decision for him, every day blending into the next, until he could no longer tell where his grief ended and her influence began.

Lena knew exactly what she was doing. She had always been a good listener, a patient one, and Jack's vulnerability was like an open invitation. She would listen to him talk about his mother—how she had been his only family, his best friend, the one person who truly understood him. He would break down, his voice cracking with emotion, and Lena would be there, always, a steady presence. She would comfort him, her words soft and soothing, telling him that he didn't have to carry the weight alone, that she was there for him.

But as Jack sank deeper into his grief, Lena became more determined to fill the void that his mother's death had left. She wasn't just comforting him anymore; she was guiding him, controlling the direction of his life. She'd casually mention how much his mother had relied on him, how she had depended on him for everything. "She was so proud of you, Jack," Lena would say, her voice a perfect blend of sympathy and understanding. "She'd want you to be strong. She'd want you to focus on the future. And I'm here to help you do that. I'm here for you."

At first, Jack was grateful. He couldn't deny that he felt an overwhelming sense of relief when she took the reins, when she made decisions for him, because the grief was too much for him to bear alone. But as time passed, he started to feel strange. The life he had known—his friends, his hobbies, his own thoughts—seemed more distant every day. It was as though he was being drawn into a world that didn't quite feel like his own, a world where Lena's voice was the only one that mattered.

One night, after yet another argument with his sister, Allison, who had come to visit to check on him, Jack found himself sitting alone in the living room, staring at the empty space beside him. He had started to notice Lena's manipulations, her gentle nudges, the way she subtly turned him against the people who cared about him. But the problem was, he didn't know how to escape. The grief still clung to him like a weight, and he wasn't sure he could navigate the world without Lena's constant presence.

That night, Lena came to him, a soft smile on her face as she sat next to him on the couch. "Jack," she whispered, "you don't need to talk to Allison. She's not what you need right now. You've always been there for her, but now it's time for you to focus on yourself. You don't have to keep carrying the burden of other people's expectations."

Jack looked at her, his heart heavy with confusion. She was right. He had always been the one to hold his family together, the one to take care of everyone else, and it felt so easy to let Lena take control. But something inside him stirred, a small voice that told him this wasn't right.

But then Lena spoke again, her voice a soothing balm. "I'm the one who's here for you, Jack. I'm the one who's been there from the beginning. Don't you see? You've always been the strong one, the responsible one. Let me take care of you now. You deserve it."

Her words wrapped around him, drawing him in again, until all he could hear was the gentle rhythm of her voice. He leaned in, resting his head on her shoulder. "I don't know what I'd do without you," he muttered, the words slipping from his lips before he could stop them.

Lena's smile deepened, a dark glint in her eyes that Jack couldn't see. He had become hers, completely and utterly, lost in the false comfort she had offered. She wasn't just comforting his grief. She was feeding off it, using it to create a life where she was the only one who mattered.

Jack never realized it, but he had been manipulated into a life he no longer recognized, with someone who had never truly loved him. And as the months passed, Lena's hold over him only tightened, until one day, when he realized that he had no one left but her, he couldn't even remember who he had been before.

The Price of Silence

Sophia had always prided herself on her secrets. Everyone had them, of course. But hers were different. Her secrets weren't just embarrassing or trivial; they were things she would never tell anyone, not even her closest friends. They were the dark corners of her life—mistakes, regrets, decisions she had made long ago that still haunted her. No one knew them. And as long as no one found out, everything would be fine.

Then she met Eliza.

Eliza was charming, confident, and a little mysterious. She was the kind of person who knew exactly how to make people feel seen, heard, understood. Sophia, a little more reserved and introverted, found herself drawn to Eliza's magnetic personality. They had met through mutual friends, and it didn't take long before they started spending more time together. Eliza made Sophia feel important, as if she was the one person who could truly get to know her, all of her. And Sophia, desperate for connection, opened up to her in ways she hadn't with anyone before.

At first, it was harmless. Eliza listened patiently, even when Sophia confessed her darkest fears and mistakes. The kind of things she'd buried deep inside herself. The relationship became intense quickly, and before long, Eliza was a constant presence in Sophia's life. They spent weekends together, confiding in one another, sharing their hopes, dreams, and yes—Sophia's secrets.

But then things started to shift. At first, it was subtle—a comment here or there about how much Eliza "understood" her. How "lucky" Sophia was to have her, because she truly knew everything about her. Sophia, ever the trusting one, smiled and brushed it off. She felt safe with Eliza, comfortable in her presence. But over time, Eliza's comments became less supportive and more insistent.

One evening, after an argument with a colleague at work, Sophia sought solace in Eliza's arms. She had always felt that Eliza was the one person who understood the pressures she was under, the loneliness that gripped her heart at times. But that night, after a brief silence between them, Eliza leaned back against the couch, eyes glinting with something darker.

"You know, Sophia," she began, her tone lighter than it had ever been before, "I've been thinking a lot about some of the things you've told me."

Sophia felt a sudden chill. She couldn't quite place it, but something in Eliza's words made her stomach drop. "What do you mean?"

"I mean," Eliza continued, leaning closer, "those things you shared with me? They're *yours*, aren't they? But they don't have to stay private. You've told me a lot of... interesting things, Sophia. Things your friends don't know. Things that could change the way people look at you. Things I could easily share."

Sophia froze, her blood running cold. "What are you talking about?"

Eliza smiled, but there was no warmth in it. "Oh, I'm just saying, I'm the only one who truly understands you, Sophia. The only one who knows all your little secrets. But what if they weren't just ours? What if everyone knew?" Her eyes gleamed with something sinister, something Sophia couldn't ignore anymore. "You'd lose everything, wouldn't you?"

The words hung in the air like a threat. Sophia's heart pounded. She could feel the weight of her darkest moments pushing against her chest. Eliza couldn't know. She couldn't.

"I'm not going to do anything, Sophia," Eliza said, her voice suddenly soft again, as if nothing had happened. "Not unless you make it worth my while."

The world seemed to tilt as the weight of what Eliza had just said sank in. Eliza wasn't threatening her out of malice, or anger. No. She was using it as leverage, a tool to manipulate Sophia into submission. She knew what could break her, knew the things that could destroy her life, and she was willing to use them to get what she wanted.

Sophia didn't sleep that night. She lay awake, staring at the ceiling, her mind racing. What had she gotten herself into? She had trusted Eliza. She had thought they were building something real. But now, Eliza wasn't the understanding friend she had once been. She was a monster wearing a friendly face, holding her past hostage.

Over the next few days, things changed. Eliza's demands started small—a request for Sophia to cancel plans with friends, to spend more time with her. Then, the requests grew. "You should quit your job. You're wasting your time. You deserve something better. Let me take care of you."

Sophia was terrified. She had already seen how far Eliza was willing to go. One day, Eliza casually mentioned the idea of moving in together. It seemed innocent enough, but Sophia knew the truth now. This wasn't about love. It was about control. Eliza had no interest in their relationship; she was just building a cage around Sophia, brick by brick, slowly suffocating her.

One evening, after another tense conversation where Eliza hinted at revealing Sophia's darkest secrets to the people she loved, Sophia snapped. "I can't keep doing this, Eliza. I won't let you use me like this anymore."

Eliza's smile didn't fade. "You don't have a choice, darling," she said, her voice cold as ice. "You'll do what I ask, or everyone will know the truth about you."

Sophia stood there, paralyzed with fear. Eliza's words rang in her ears, and for a moment, she saw everything clearly. Eliza wasn't just threatening her; she was feeding off her fear, her insecurities. She was using the weight of Sophia's past to control every aspect of her life.

And then, just as quickly as it had started, a thought flickered in Sophia's mind, one that terrified her. If she walked away, if she refused to comply, Eliza would destroy her. But if she stayed... if she continued to allow Eliza to control her, to manipulate her, what would be left of her? What kind of life would she be living?

The answer came to her in the darkest of moments. It didn't matter what Eliza threatened anymore. She had already lost herself. She wasn't just afraid of losing her secrets. She was afraid of losing everything else: her dignity, her independence, her sense of self.

But by the time she realized it, it was too late. Eliza's grip was already too tight. The secret had already been revealed to someone else. And in that moment, Sophia knew that Eliza had always held the power. She hadn't just manipulated her. She had *made* her.

The Quiet Collapse

Emma had always been ambitious. When she first met Rachel, she saw in her the kind of strength she admired—confident, driven, independent. Rachel was the kind of woman who seemed to have it all together, effortlessly climbing the corporate ladder with a smile. She had a natural charm that drew people in, a way of making everyone feel comfortable in her presence. And for a while, Emma felt lucky. She was in awe of Rachel's success, and she admired her work ethic. They made the perfect couple—two strong women, each in control of their own destiny, working together, living together, dreaming together.

But after the first few months of their relationship, something started to shift. Emma began to notice the little things—the way Rachel would make a comment about her job, her colleagues, the projects she was working on. "I don't know why you haven't gotten the promotion yet," Rachel would say casually, a glass of wine in her hand. "You're way smarter than any of them. But I guess they just don't see it, huh?"

Rachel's words were meant to be comforting, but something about them made Emma uneasy. She could hear the subtle implication—was she not good enough? Was her hard work not enough to be recognized? At first, she ignored it, but the feeling lingered. Over time, the comments became more frequent, more pointed. "I don't know why you keep getting passed over, Emma. Maybe you just need to be more like me. You know, more... assertive."

Emma would smile, trying to push the discomfort away, but the seeds had been planted. Rachel had always been supportive, or at least she pretended to be, but now Emma began to notice the small ways Rachel would undermine her. At dinner with friends, Rachel would talk about Emma's job, sharing details Emma hadn't even realized she'd shared, and always framing it in a way that made Emma seem uncertain, indecisive. She was never malicious, but there was always a subtle hint that Emma wasn't living up to her potential, that maybe she wasn't trying hard enough.

One evening, as Emma sat in the living room, papers scattered around her as she worked through another late-night presentation, Rachel wandered in with a glass of water. She looked at the papers, her eyes scanning them without any real interest. "You know," she said softly, "I don't understand why you're doing all this extra work. The boss already told you he wasn't impressed with your last proposal. Why keep going?"

Emma froze, her fingers stilling on the keyboard. The sting of Rachel's words was sharper than it should have been. Rachel had always been a little too candid, a little too blunt with her opinions. "I'm just trying to prove myself," Emma said, her voice quieter than she intended.

Rachel's smile was sympathetic, but it didn't reach her eyes. "You don't have to try so hard. If they don't see your worth, why waste your energy? It's not like they're going to give you that promotion anytime soon, right?"

The words hung in the air, poisoning the room with doubt. Emma tried to push them away, but they stayed with her long after Rachel left the room. The next day at work, the words echoed in her mind as she prepared for a meeting. She'd been working on this presentation for weeks, pouring everything she had into it, hoping this would be the moment that would prove her worth. But as she stood in front of her team, explaining the project, she could feel the weight of Rachel's words bearing down on her.

Her colleagues' faces were unreadable, their eyes flicking to their phones as she spoke. She fumbled through the slides, her words becoming jumbled, her confidence faltering. The meeting ended in a hushed silence, and as Emma sat back at her desk, she could already feel the cold reality settling in. No one was impressed. No one cared.

Over the following weeks, the sabotage continued, though it was always cloaked in the guise of concern or advice. "Maybe you should stop trying so hard to be liked by everyone," Rachel would suggest when Emma came home, drained from another day of rejection. "You don't need their approval. You just need to focus on what's best for you, not them."

But there was always a catch. The advice was never empowering. It was always subtly undermining, making Emma question herself, making her second-guess every decision she made at work. Rachel didn't have to say much. It was the way she looked at Emma when she came home with news about her day—the way she would sigh when Emma spoke about a project she was excited about, as if it was a burden.

Emma's self-doubt grew. Her confidence at work evaporated, replaced by a constant, gnawing fear that she wasn't good enough. She found herself struggling to make decisions, questioning everything she did. The meetings she used to lead with ease now felt like insurmountable obstacles. The weight of Rachel's words, the constant undermining, had left her paralyzed.

One day, after another humiliating meeting, Emma returned home early, hoping to find solace in Rachel's arms. She needed reassurance, needed someone to tell her that she was still capable, that she wasn't as worthless as she felt. But when she walked through the door, Rachel wasn't there.

It was a few hours later when Rachel returned, her face tight with frustration. "Why are you home so early?" she asked, her tone colder than usual.

"I couldn't focus," Emma said, her voice barely above a whisper. "Everything's falling apart, Rachel. I don't know what I'm doing wrong."

Rachel's gaze was icy as she walked past Emma, dropping her coat on the couch. "You've been saying that for weeks now," she said. "Maybe it's time to face reality, Emma. You're just not cut out for this. Maybe you should quit before they fire you."

Emma's chest tightened as her heart sank. "What are you talking about?" she whispered, the words barely escaping her lips. "You know I can't quit. I've worked so hard for this. I need this job."

Rachel's eyes narrowed. "You need me, Emma. Not the job. Not the company. Me. I'm the one who's been there for you, who's helped you see the truth. You'll never be good enough for them. But with me, you'll be fine. Don't you see? I've been trying to help you avoid failure."

It was then that Emma realized the truth she had been too blind to see. Rachel wasn't just offering advice; she was breaking her down. She was pushing her to the edge, slowly, quietly, until Emma was too weak to stand on her own. Every comment, every look, every whispered word had been part of a plan—Rachel's plan to strip Emma of her confidence, to make her dependent on her. Rachel wasn't trying to help Emma succeed. She was making sure Emma would always need her, always rely on her for validation.

As the days passed, Emma sank further into despair. The self-doubt Rachel had nurtured in her grew into something far worse. Her career, her sense of self, everything she had worked for was unraveling. And the worst part? She couldn't escape it. Rachel had made sure of that.

The Price of Devotion

When Natalie first met Lena, she felt like she had finally found someone who understood her. They clicked instantly. Lena was smart, confident, and seemingly perfect—everything that Natalie had been searching for. It wasn't long before they were inseparable, spending all their time together, talking about everything from childhood memories to their deepest fears. Lena listened attentively, never judging, and Natalie felt an overwhelming sense of safety in her presence. For the first time in a long while, she felt truly seen.

But as their relationship grew deeper, Natalie began to notice small things—insinuations, questions about her past, her past lovers, her most painful memories. At first, it seemed harmless. Lena would ask about Natalie's ex-boyfriend, a relationship that ended badly. "What happened between you two?" Lena would ask casually, her voice soft and understanding. "You don't have to tell me everything, of course. But it must have been hard."

At first, Natalie had no problem talking about it. She wasn't ashamed of her past, and Lena's curiosity felt like it came from a place of love and genuine interest. But soon, the questions began to feel more like a probe, more like an examination of her weaknesses. Lena would ask about past friendships, family dynamics, things Natalie had long buried.

"Tell me about your childhood," Lena asked one evening. "I just want to know everything about you."

Natalie hesitated. She had a complicated relationship with her parents, particularly her mother, whose judgmental attitude had left deep scars on Natalie's self-esteem. It was a subject she rarely brought up. But Lena was persistent. She looked at Natalie with those big, empathetic eyes, and Natalie found herself spilling the most intimate parts of her life.

As Lena continued to gain access to the deepest corners of Natalie's mind, she began to change. She became more possessive, more controlling. At first, it seemed like affection. She'd call Natalie constantly, checking in on her, making sure she was okay. "I just want to make sure you're safe," she'd say, her voice laced with concern.

But as the weeks passed, it became clear that this was more than just concern—it was control. Lena began to dictate where Natalie went, who she talked to, even what she wore. "You don't need to see your friends as much," Lena would say, "They don't understand us. We're all you need."

And for a while, Natalie believed it. The isolation was subtle, but it was there. Slowly, Lena replaced everyone in Natalie's life. Her friends, her family, they all faded into the background as Lena became her entire world.

But it wasn't until Lena started using the things Natalie had shared against her that the full extent of her manipulation became clear. It started innocently enough—small things that didn't seem to matter at first. When Natalie would voice a small disagreement, Lena would remind her of her past mistakes, using them as a way to silence her.

"You remember what happened last time you were this stubborn?" Lena would say. "You almost ruined everything. Do you really want to go down that road again?"

At first, it was just words. Natalie tried to brush it off, but over time, Lena's threats became more pointed, more chilling. One evening, after a disagreement over something trivial, Lena came to Natalie, her eyes cold and calculating.

"You're really pushing me, you know," Lena said, her voice low and dangerous. "You don't want to make me angry. I have so much on you, things you've never told anyone."

Natalie's blood ran cold. She tried to laugh it off, to pretend it was just another one of Lena's manipulative games. But Lena wasn't joking.

"I know about your ex. The one you cheated on," Lena said, her voice smooth as silk. "I know about the things you did when you were younger, things you've never told anyone. Things you've buried so deep, you think no one remembers. But I remember."

Natalie's heart raced. Her stomach churned with a sickening realization. Lena wasn't just trying to control her; she was blackmailing her. She had been collecting her darkest secrets all along, using them as leverage to get what she wanted.

Lena's smile widened as she saw the fear in Natalie's eyes. "You don't want me to tell your friends about that night, do you? You don't want them to know about the things you've done. About how you really feel about your mother. About your real feelings towards your old job."

Natalie's throat tightened. "You wouldn't do that," she whispered, but the doubt was there. She had seen the power Lena had over her, seen how easily she could manipulate the people around her.

Lena's eyes gleamed. "Don't worry, darling. I won't do anything unless you make me."

The next few days felt like a fog. Natalie couldn't think straight. She felt trapped, suffocated by the weight of Lena's control. She was paralyzed by fear—fear that if she didn't comply with Lena's every whim, if she didn't stay obedient, the truth would come out. She couldn't lose Lena, but at the same time, she couldn't bear the thought of her darkest secrets being exposed to the world.

Lena continued to tighten her grip. She told Natalie how to behave at work, how to interact with her colleagues, and most chillingly, who she was allowed to speak to. "Your friends are bad influences," Lena would say, "They just want to tear us apart. They don't understand how important we are."

But as the days passed, Natalie's mind began to unravel. The constant threat of exposure, the emotional manipulation, the isolation—it all became too much. She was losing herself. She couldn't remember the last time she'd done something just for herself, the last time she'd made a decision without Lena's influence.

One evening, Natalie came home after a long day of trying to appease Lena's every demand. She collapsed onto the couch, exhausted and defeated. Lena was there, as always, waiting for her.

"You know what happens if you don't follow through, right?" Lena asked, her voice soft but deadly.

Natalie's heart raced, but this time, something inside her broke. She could feel the walls closing in, and suddenly, she was sick of it. She had given Lena everything—her love, her trust, her secrets—and now, she had nothing left.

"I can't do this anymore," Natalie whispered, her voice barely audible.

Lena's smile faded. She stepped closer, her eyes cold. "You don't have a choice, Natalie. I own you now."

In that moment, something inside Natalie snapped. She had been living in fear for so long, but she realized she was no longer afraid of Lena. She wasn't afraid of the threats, the blackmail, the power Lena had over her.

She stood up, trembling with rage, and walked towards the door. Lena didn't move, but there was a flicker of doubt in her eyes.

"I'm leaving," Natalie said, her voice shaking but firm. "You can't control me anymore. Your power over me is gone."

Lena's face twisted in anger. "You'll regret this. I'll ruin you."

But Natalie didn't care anymore. She opened the door and walked out, her mind finally free.

As she stepped into the night, a sense of clarity washed over her. She had finally broken free. And in the silence that followed, she realized that Lena had always been the prisoner—prisoner to her own need for control, to her own fear of losing someone who had once trusted her.

But now, it was Lena who was alone. And this time, Natalie knew she wouldn't look back.

Torn Threads

Megan had never intended to fall for Tom. When she first met him, he seemed like a kind, sensitive man—someone who had been through his own share of pain but was strong enough to carry on. His children were a part of him, of course, but they had never seemed to be anything more than an afterthought in their early days together. She saw in him someone who had rebuilt his life after a divorce and was now looking for peace and companionship. He wasn't perfect, but neither was she, and they fit together like pieces of a puzzle—until they didn't.

It started small, as most things do, with subtle shifts that went unnoticed until they had become impossible to ignore. Megan had always been independent, her own life built on her career, her friendships, her dreams of being more than just someone's partner. But when she moved in with Tom, things began to change. His ex-wife, Claire, had been a significant part of the picture, and Megan told herself it was normal to share a life with someone who had children. She told herself that it was just a matter of finding the balance.

The first time she had noticed something was wrong was after a family weekend with Tom's two children, Lily and Ben. They were teenagers, bright and outspoken, but still a little rough around the edges. She'd spent the day helping them with their homework, trying to connect with them, hoping they'd see her as someone they could rely on. That night, as they all sat down for dinner, the phone rang. Tom answered it, his tone sharp as he spoke with Claire. Megan caught a few words, but what struck her was the silence that followed the conversation, a heaviness that she couldn't shake.

That night, Tom didn't speak much. He didn't apologize, didn't explain. But the next day, things began to shift. Megan would find herself doing more for the children—more than she had ever expected to do. Tom would give her little smiles of appreciation, but there was an underlying message that she began to sense: this was expected of her. It was part of the job now, and she was supposed to be the one to keep everything running smoothly, to make sure the children didn't feel abandoned. She had become the caretaker, the one who made sure things were "okay."

Over time, the tension between Megan and Claire grew, a quiet undercurrent of hostility that no one dared to speak about but everyone felt. Claire would call during dinner, always checking in on the children, always questioning Megan's decisions. She would make comments about what she thought was best for the kids, even when it had nothing to do with her. And Tom, for reasons Megan could never understand, would rarely step in. His loyalty to his ex-wife was silent but ever-present. Megan had begun to feel like an outsider in her own relationship.

But it wasn't until the incident with Ben that Megan truly understood the dynamic she had stepped into.

Ben had been acting out at school, skipping classes and hanging out with a group of kids who were known for trouble. Megan tried talking to him, tried to get him to open up, but he shut her down. Tom seemed indifferent, as if he was too tired to deal with it. Claire, on the other hand, stepped in with her usual "mother knows best" approach. It was the first time Megan had truly seen the full extent of Claire's control over her family, and she hadn't liked it.

The next day, Tom called Megan into the living room. His face was pale, his eyes strained. "Claire thinks you're being too hard on Ben," he said, his voice low. "She thinks you're not giving him enough space. You know, with everything he's been through..."

Megan's heart sank. She knew exactly what he meant, but she couldn't help herself. She had been trying to be there for Ben, to make sure he didn't fall through the cracks. But it was always the same. Claire's influence seemed to weigh more heavily than anything Megan said or did. "I'm just trying to help him, Tom," Megan said, feeling her voice crack. "He's not just going to figure it out on his own. He needs boundaries."

Tom didn't answer. He just looked at her, the silence pressing down on both of them. Megan's stomach twisted. She had tried, tried so hard, to fit into this family, to be the stepmother, to be what they needed. But each time she reached out, Claire's shadow was always there, pulling the strings.

Days passed. The tension grew. Tom grew quieter, more distant. Claire's calls became more frequent, more pointed. Each time, Megan found herself second-guessing her every move. The weight of her failures, her shortcomings as a partner and a stepmother, were slowly wearing her down.

Then came the conversation that shattered everything.

It was a Sunday evening, and Megan and Tom had been arguing about something trivial. The kids had been fighting, Tom had been distracted, and nothing seemed to be going right. She tried to talk to him about how she was feeling—how she was tired, how she felt like she was doing everything but still wasn't good enough—but he didn't listen. Instead, he looked at her with a mixture of exhaustion and something colder, something more calculated.

"You know, Megan," he said, his voice quiet but cutting, "maybe you should reconsider this whole thing. You've been great with the kids, but if it's too much for you, Claire will gladly step in and do it all. I don't think you're cut out for it."

The words hit her like a slap. He had said it so calmly, so without emotion. He was just stating a fact. Claire would step in. Claire always did.

Megan stood there, her world unraveling around her. She had never felt so small, so powerless. All of her efforts, all of her care, had been for nothing. She was just a placeholder, a temporary solution until Claire could come back and "fix" everything.

She tried to speak, to explain, to fight back. But as she did, she realized something worse. Tom wasn't even trying to defend her. He wasn't trying to make her feel like she mattered. He had already made up his mind. And Claire's grip on their family was just too strong.

The next day, Megan packed her things. She had never felt more alone, more broken. She knew that leaving would mean giving up on the family she had tried to build, but staying meant living in a world where she would never be enough. Claire would always be there, lurking in the shadows, and Tom would never be the partner she needed.

Megan left, but as she walked away, she couldn't shake the thought that perhaps, in the end, she had always been nothing more than a pawn in someone else's game. And no matter what she did, no matter how much she tried to give, the threads that bound her to them would never be hers to cut.

The Weight of Her Love

Amelia was everything Sarah had ever wanted. They met at a coffee shop on a rainy afternoon, both of them seeking refuge from the storm. Amelia had an infectious laugh, a way of lighting up a room just by being in it. Sarah, quiet and introspective, found herself drawn to Amelia's energy. She admired the way Amelia could make everything feel effortless, her confidence like a beacon in Sarah's more reserved world.

At first, their relationship was full of joy. They spent their weekends together, talking for hours about everything and nothing. Amelia shared her dreams, her passions, her fears, and Sarah listened, eager to be the one who supported her. Amelia had a way of making Sarah feel important, needed. The more Sarah gave, the more Amelia seemed to open up, and Sarah found herself falling deeper in love with the woman who made her feel like she was the center of the universe.

But over time, things began to change. At first, it was small things—little requests for help, a few late-night phone calls when Amelia was feeling down. Sarah didn't mind. She loved being there for Amelia, loved the idea that she could be someone's constant support. But as the months passed, the requests became more frequent, more urgent. Amelia seemed to always be in crisis, always needing someone to hold her together.

One night, after Sarah had come home from a long day at work, Amelia called her in tears. "I don't know what to do, Sarah. I'm just... falling apart," she sobbed.

Sarah's stomach sank. "What happened?"

"I lost my job today. They just... they just let me go, and I don't know how I'm going to pay the rent, how I'm going to... I can't do this alone. Please, you have to help me."

Sarah's heart ached. She dropped her purse on the floor and sank onto the couch, her mind already racing through the steps of how to help. "We'll figure it out. I'll help you with your resume, I'll cover the rent if we need to. We'll get through this together."

For the next few weeks, Sarah was there, tirelessly supporting Amelia as she navigated her unemployment. Every time Sarah thought she could take a breath, there would be another call, another crisis. Amelia's mood swings became more pronounced. Some days, she was upbeat and optimistic, while other days, she was consumed by despair. Sarah didn't know how to handle it. She just knew that Amelia needed her. And that need consumed Sarah's every waking moment.

But then, one day, the tables turned. Amelia didn't ask for help. Instead, she simply stared at Sarah from across the table, her face blank.

"I think we need to talk," Amelia said, her voice soft but firm.

"What's wrong?" Sarah asked, her heart tightening in her chest.

"I can't do this anymore, Sarah. I feel like I'm suffocating. You're smothering me."

Sarah froze, her mind racing. "What do you mean? I've been helping you. I've been here for you, every step of the way."

Amelia leaned back in her chair, folding her arms across her chest. "I know you're trying to help, but you're always here, always trying to fix everything. I never have any space. You're always there when I need you, and it's too much. I need to breathe. I need some independence."

The words felt like a slap to Sarah's face. She had given everything to Amelia, had poured her heart into this relationship, and now, Amelia was telling her that it was too much. Sarah's chest tightened with a mix of confusion and hurt. "I'm just trying to be there for you. You said you needed me. You said you couldn't do this without me."

Amelia sighed, rubbing her temples. "I know, I know. But it's just... it's draining. I can't keep depending on you for everything. I feel like I'm losing myself in all of this. I don't even know who I am anymore."

The words echoed in Sarah's mind, her heart breaking with each one. She had spent months holding Amelia up, making her feel needed, wanted. And now, it felt like it was all unraveling.

But just as quickly as it had come, Amelia softened, her voice quieter now. "I'm sorry, Sarah. I didn't mean it like that. I just... I'm overwhelmed. I love you, but I don't know how to manage everything. I need you to understand that."

Sarah nodded, swallowing her hurt. She understood. She had to. She loved Amelia too much to do anything else.

Over the next few weeks, the cycle continued. Amelia would sink into a new crisis, and Sarah would be there, picking up the pieces. But now, the cracks in their relationship were impossible to ignore. Every time Amelia needed her, Sarah would drop everything, putting her own needs aside. But it wasn't just the crisis moments. Amelia started controlling the everyday aspects of Sarah's life, too.

"Don't go out with your friends tonight," Amelia would say. "I need you here."

"I'll cancel," Sarah would reply, guilt flooding her. "I'll be here for you."

And it went on, this silent, insidious dance, where Amelia's crises became Sarah's entire world. The guilt, the need to fix everything, kept Sarah in a constant state of exhaustion. And no matter how much she gave, it was never enough.

One night, after yet another emotional breakdown from Amelia, Sarah sat on the couch, staring blankly at the wall. Amelia was in the kitchen, making a cup of tea, her back to Sarah. For the first time, Sarah allowed herself to think about what had been happening. She had been so focused on fixing Amelia's life that she had lost herself. She was drowning in the weight of someone else's chaos. And what had she gotten in return? Nothing but exhaustion, guilt, and the constant fear that if she wasn't there, everything would fall apart.

The realization hit her like a ton of bricks. She had allowed herself to be consumed by this relationship, to become a shadow of the person she once was. She had thought that loving Amelia meant sacrificing everything, but now, she wasn't sure who she was anymore.

When Amelia returned to the living room, her tea in hand, she looked at Sarah with those pleading eyes. "I'm sorry, Sarah. I didn't mean to do this to you. I just don't know how to handle everything."

Sarah's voice was barely a whisper as she looked at her. "I can't do this anymore, Amelia. I can't keep giving and giving when you never let me breathe."

Amelia's face fell, and for a moment, Sarah saw the vulnerability, the fear that had always been there beneath the surface. But it was too late. The exhaustion, the emotional drain, had taken its toll.

"I don't know how to fix this," Sarah said, her voice trembling. "But I know I can't keep losing myself to you."

And as she walked out the door that night, leaving behind a woman who would never truly see her, Sarah understood. She had never been loved for who she was. She had been loved for what she could give. And now, in the silence that followed, she realized the darkest truth: love, when it demands everything and offers nothing in return, is the cruelest manipulation of all.

The Quiet Heart

Lena had always been drawn to people who needed help. It wasn't just her empathy that led her to become a caregiver by profession; it was a deep-seated need to fix, to heal, to feel like she was doing something important. Her life, for as long as she could remember, had been about others—making them feel cared for, needed, worthy of attention. So, when she met Oliver, she saw someone who, like so many others, needed fixing.

Oliver was charming, kind, with a smile that could light up a room, but underneath the surface, there was an undeniable sadness in him. He had been through losses, disappointments, and the kind of pain that seemed to linger in his eyes. He told her about his difficult childhood, the estranged relationship with his parents, the string of failed friendships that had left him isolated. But when he was with her, Lena could see the potential for healing. She could help him, make him whole again.

At first, it felt easy. Oliver would call her when he was feeling low, and Lena would drop everything to comfort him. She became his safe space, his anchor. He was so fragile, so lost, and she felt herself growing more and more indispensable with each passing day. The first time he cried in front of her, Lena promised herself she would never let him feel that alone again. She began to see their relationship as a rescue mission—a mission that she alone could fulfill.

The more she helped him, the more Oliver seemed to lean on her. He leaned on her emotionally, physically, and in every way that mattered. He would apologize for his behavior when he withdrew into himself or lashed out. "I'm sorry, Lena. I don't mean to push you away," he would say. "It's just... I don't know how to cope sometimes."

And Lena, ever the caretaker, reassured him, forgave him, and continued to offer her support. But over time, the lines between being a support system and being a prisoner started to blur. Oliver's apologies became less frequent, his behavior more demanding. He started to expect that she would always be there, that her life would revolve around him and his needs.

Lena's world shrank as she gave more and more of herself to him. She stopped seeing her friends, stopped going to the gym, stopped taking time for herself. Every minute of her life became about Oliver—his pain, his needs, his healing. She thought she was helping him, that she was being a good partner, but slowly, insidiously, she began to lose herself in the process.

The pattern became familiar: Oliver would experience a new crisis, some fresh disappointment or personal failure, and Lena would rush to his side, doing everything she could to console him. But the more she gave, the more Oliver took. It wasn't long before she noticed the shift—the shift in how she felt around him.

One evening, after yet another exhausting day of comforting Oliver through a breakdown, Lena sat quietly in their small living room. She was tired, her body aching from the constant strain of his emotional weight. She had given so much, and yet Oliver's pain seemed endless. He sat beside her, his head on her shoulder, playing the role of the fragile, broken man. His voice was low, shaky.

"You're the only one who gets me, Lena," he whispered. "I don't know what I'd do without you."

The words sounded genuine, sincere, but there was something in the way he said them that made Lena uneasy. His hand lingered on hers, just a little too long, like a constant reminder that he was dependent on her, that he needed her more than anyone else. It wasn't just love anymore. It was suffocation, and Lena was the one being slowly suffocated.

That night, after Oliver had fallen asleep, Lena stayed awake, her mind racing. She thought about all the promises she had made to herself before she met him. She had wanted to travel, to build her own career, to have space for her own desires. But now, all of that seemed so distant, so irrelevant. She was living for him, for his pain, his drama. And somehow, it was never enough.

Weeks passed, and Lena's exhaustion deepened. Oliver's crises were escalating, and every time she thought things were stabilizing, something new would emerge. It was always something. The stress of his work, his family, his old friends—it never stopped. And Lena, ever the dutiful partner, kept giving. She kept rescuing, patching him up, convincing him that he was worthy, that he wasn't a burden. But the more she gave, the more she saw the cracks in the façade.

One evening, after a particularly draining weekend where Oliver had spiraled into a depressive state, Lena couldn't take it anymore. She had tried everything—calming words, soothing touches, quiet assurances—but it was never enough. As she watched him curled up on the couch, his eyes blank and distant, she realized something horrifying: Oliver wasn't trying to get better. He was playing the victim.

Lena had been so wrapped up in her role as his savior that she hadn't seen the manipulation unfolding before her. Every time he cried, every time he demanded her attention, he wasn't just grieving. He was using her, using her need to help as a means of control. He wasn't broken in the way he led her to believe—he was simply taking advantage of her love, of her devotion. And she had let him.

The realization hit her like a slap. He wasn't healing, and neither was she. She had become trapped in his web of emotional dependency. And yet, as much as she wanted to walk away, she knew she couldn't. Not yet.

That night, after he had fallen asleep again, Lena sat in the dark, staring at the empty space between them on the couch. She realized with a sickening clarity that everything she had done—the sacrifices, the sleepless nights, the constant giving—it had all been a way for Oliver to keep her where he wanted her: desperate, needed, unable to leave.

The next day, Lena tried to confront him. She told him she couldn't continue, that the emotional toll was too much for her. She needed space, time for herself. Oliver's response was everything she feared. He looked at her, his eyes wide and hurt, and said the words that tore through her heart: "You would leave me, wouldn't you? After everything I've shared with you? You would abandon me now, when I need you most? You'd be just like everyone else."

His voice trembled with such vulnerability, such self-pity, that Lena's resolve faltered. She couldn't abandon him. Couldn't be the bad person. Not after everything he had shared, not after everything he had convinced her she had to do.

And so, despite every bone in her body screaming for freedom, Lena stayed. She stayed in the prison she had built for herself, a prison forged from Oliver's manipulation and her own guilt. She stayed because she didn't know how to leave.

In the end, Lena had become the victim, too—trapped in a cycle of emotional torment, quietly destroyed by her own devotion. And the worst part was, she knew she would never be able to escape. Not while Oliver needed her to stay.

The Chains of Affection

It had been months since Olivia moved in with me, but it felt like we had been together for years. In the beginning, everything seemed perfect. She was warm, attentive, and always seemed to know exactly what I needed. She listened when I spoke, laughed at my jokes, and made me feel like the most important person in the room. I had never known love could feel this effortless.

But slowly, as the days wore on, I began to feel the walls close in. It started small—a comment here, a suggestion there. Olivia would casually say things like, "I don't think you should go out tonight, babe. You've been so busy lately. You need to rest." Or, "Do you really need to see your friends again this week? You're always so tired after hanging out with them."

At first, I didn't mind. She was just looking out for me, right? She wanted what was best for me. She wanted to protect me from the stress of the world, from the overwhelming demands of work and social obligations. She was my support, my anchor, and I was grateful.

But as time passed, those small requests began to feel like demands. The nights I used to spend with my friends became fewer. The trips to see my family started to feel like chores, like something I had to apologize for. Olivia would look at me with those pleading eyes whenever I tried to make plans without her. "Don't you want to spend more time with me? We don't get enough time together. I miss you," she would say, her voice soft, sweet, but the undertone of guilt was always there.

It wasn't just the time. It was everything. The way I dressed, the way I spent my money, the way I organized my life. She would always have an opinion. "That shirt looks too casual," she'd say, pulling at the fabric with her fingers. "Why don't you try something a little more elegant? You want people to take you seriously, don't you?"

"Maybe you should rethink that purchase," she'd murmur as I added something to the cart online. "You don't need it. What if we put that money toward something we'll both enjoy?"

I began to lose track of what I truly liked, what made me feel good. Her preferences, her rules, her opinions—slowly, they started to become my own. Every time I made a decision, I would ask myself, "What would Olivia think? What would make her happy?" And the more I thought like that, the more my independence slipped away.

I had become someone else—a version of myself that was filtered through her eyes, shaped by her wants, her needs, her desires. I didn't even notice it happening until one day, when I tried to plan something on my own again, and Olivia stopped me before I could even make a move.

"I don't think you should do that," she said, her tone calm but firm, her hand on my arm like a tether. "It's just not a good idea. You don't want to hurt anyone's feelings, do you? What if they don't understand? What if they think you don't care about them?"

Her voice, so gentle and persuasive, made my thoughts spin. I looked at her, confused. What was I doing? She was right, wasn't she? Of course, I couldn't go through with it. I couldn't risk anyone thinking that I was selfish, that I was abandoning the people I loved. I couldn't risk her being disappointed in me.

And so, I stopped planning things entirely. I gave up any illusion of independence. I let Olivia make every decision for me, from the mundane to the significant. I thought it was love. I thought this was what it meant to be cared for—to have someone who loved you so much that they wanted to make sure you never made a mistake, never felt alone, never had to think for yourself. It felt like devotion.

But the truth was darker than that.

One evening, after another week of watching Olivia steer me in every direction, I found myself sitting in front of a mirror, studying my face. The reflection staring back at me seemed foreign, like someone I barely knew. My hair, my clothes, my posture—none of it felt like me. I had become a stranger to myself.

I thought about the things I had given up. The spontaneous trips, the nights out with friends, the conversations about things that weren't related to Olivia or us. I had stopped reading books I loved because Olivia didn't like them. I had stopped going to places I used to love because she didn't like them either.

But now, in the silence of that moment, I could hear it—the soft, insidious voice in the back of my mind that had been growing louder for months. *This isn't love. This isn't freedom. This is a prison.*

I shook the thought away, but it lingered. I wasn't sure where it had come from. I hadn't been unhappy, not really. But somewhere, in the deepest part of me, I knew something was wrong. The constant surveillance of my every move, the way my life seemed to revolve around her approval, the way I felt like a puppet on a string—it was suffocating.

Then the next day, as I was sitting on the couch with Olivia, a text message came through on my phone. It was from my best friend, Laura—someone I hadn't heard from in weeks. She asked if I was free for lunch next weekend, if we could catch up.

I hesitated, my fingers hovering over the screen. I wanted to say yes, wanted to feel like myself again. But then I looked at Olivia. Her eyes were on me, those expectant eyes that always seemed to know what I was thinking, and I felt that familiar pull—like a rope tightening around my chest.

"You should tell her you're busy," Olivia said softly, her voice just the right balance of caring and directive. "You don't need to be out there with her. You know how much she talks. You'll just get caught up in something you don't need."

My heart sank. I looked at the message on my phone, then back at Olivia, and in that moment, the truth hit me like a ton of bricks. This was no longer love. This was control, disguised as affection. She had turned every aspect of my life into a sacrifice, twisting every desire, every thought, into something that revolved around her. She wasn't just loving me—she was keeping me small. She was slowly, quietly erasing me.

I typed a reply to Laura, telling her I couldn't make it. Then I put the phone down and smiled at Olivia. But inside, something had snapped. The love I thought I'd been living for was just another cage, and the worst part was that I had locked myself inside it.

And so, as the days continued to pass, I felt myself becoming more and more invisible, fading into the background of the life she had built for both of us. But in that quiet emptiness, I realized: I hadn't just lost myself. I had given myself away, piece by piece, in exchange for a love that was nothing more than a prison.

The Final Choice

Leah had always been someone who loved deeply. She gave herself wholeheartedly in every relationship—whether it was with friends, family, or lovers. She believed that love was about balance, about sharing the best parts of yourself with others and having them do the same in return. When she met Clara, she thought she had found someone who understood that, someone who matched her passion for connection. Clara was everything Leah had wanted in a partner: warm, engaging, and seemingly full of life.

In the beginning, everything felt perfect. Clara was supportive, always interested in what Leah was doing, always willing to share her own world with her. They spent weekends together, going on long walks, sharing quiet evenings, laughing over silly inside jokes. But as the months passed, Leah started to notice something darker lurking beneath the surface.

It started with small comments. Clara would make little remarks about Leah's friendships, subtle jabs that didn't seem malicious at first but began to eat away at her confidence. "You always spend so much time with Sarah," Clara would say one evening, her voice light but edged with something else. "I know you've been friends for years, but sometimes it feels like you care more about her than me."

Leah would brush it off. Sarah had been her best friend since college. She was like family. But the comments kept coming. And then, Clara began to suggest that Leah's family, too, took up too much of her time. "Why do you need to go visit your parents every weekend? I thought you and I had plans for this weekend."

"I told you I would be there for them," Leah would respond, trying to explain herself. "You know how important they are to me."

Clara would look disappointed, but she'd never push it too far. "I just feel like they always come first. You never put us first." There it was again, that quiet accusation.

Leah felt a pang in her chest, but she tried to ignore it. She loved Clara, and maybe she was overthinking things. Clara had always been open about her needs, and maybe this was just her way of asking for more. Maybe she needed more of Leah's time, more of her attention.

But it wasn't just the comments. It was the way Clara started controlling their social life, dictating who they spent time with. Whenever Leah would suggest meeting up with friends, Clara would make a point of being "busy," withdrawing into herself. "I don't know if I want to hang out with them again, Leah. They've been really critical of us. You should spend more time with me. You deserve to focus on what really matters."

Leah's world began to shrink. She started cancelling plans with friends, making excuses to not see her family, all because Clara's needs always seemed more urgent. Every time Leah questioned it, Clara would respond with a quiet, almost too understanding expression. "I just feel like I'm losing you, Leah. You say you love me, but I don't see it when you prioritize everyone else over me."

The guilt was overwhelming. Leah didn't want to lose Clara. She loved her deeply, and Clara's vulnerabilities had begun to feel like a weight on Leah's shoulders. Every time she saw the disappointment in Clara's eyes, it became harder to go against her wishes. The tug-of-war between Clara and the people who had once been her closest companions became unbearable.

One evening, after a particularly tense argument about a dinner date Leah had planned with her parents, Clara confronted her with a chilling ultimatum. "You need to decide, Leah. I can't keep going like this. It's either me or them."

Leah froze, feeling the walls closing in. She had never been in this situation before—where love felt like an obligation, where every action she took seemed to betray someone. "What do you mean?" she asked, her voice trembling.

Clara's gaze was sharp, almost calculating. "I'm tired of being the second choice. I'm tired of always being told that everyone else is more important than me. You can't have both, Leah. You can't have me and your family, your friends. You have to choose."

The words hung in the air, suffocating her. Leah knew that Clara wasn't just asking for more time. She was asking for control. She wanted Leah to sever ties with the people she had loved long before Clara entered her life. And the worst part was that Leah could feel herself being pulled in. The idea of losing Clara—of losing the one person who seemed to understand her in ways no one else did—made her heart ache.

"I don't want to choose," Leah whispered.

But Clara's response was swift, cutting through the room like a knife. "You already have. You've already chosen them over me time and time again. I just need you to admit it."

That night, Leah barely slept. She tossed and turned, trying to imagine her life without Clara, trying to picture a future where she could still be the person she had once been, where she could still care for the people who had always supported her. But Clara's words echoed in her mind, the quiet insistence that she was the one who mattered, the one who deserved all of Leah's devotion. The guilt of it all made Leah physically ill.

The next day, Clara was distant, her eyes cold and her words clipped. "I'll give you some time to think about it, but don't take too long, Leah. I don't want to be in a relationship where I'm constantly second best. I deserve someone who puts me first."

Leah felt her heart shatter as the weight of the decision pressed down on her. She sat in her apartment that night, staring at the phone, trying to find the words to tell her family, to tell Sarah, what was happening. But she couldn't. She had already promised Clara that she would choose.

By morning, she had made her choice. It wasn't that she didn't love her family or her friends. But Clara needed her in a way they didn't. Clara was fragile, and Sarah and her parents had never truly understood that. Leah had to protect what they had, even if it meant sacrificing everything else.

She sent the text. "I can't see you all today. I'm with Clara. I need to stay with her. I'm sorry." The words felt like a betrayal, but they felt necessary.

Clara's smile that evening was radiant, a mask of relief that made Leah's stomach turn. "I knew you'd make the right choice," she said, pulling Leah into an embrace that felt tighter than it should have.

But as Leah stood there, in the arms of the woman she loved, she realized something terrifying. The choice she had made had been hers, yes—but the decision had already been made for her. Clara had won. And in the process, she had taken more than just Leah's time, her friends, or her family. She had taken her sense of self, her independence, her freedom.

And the worst part was, Leah didn't even know if she could find it again.

The Lies We Live

Emma had always been the strong one. The dependable one. The friend who kept everyone grounded, the partner who held things together when life threatened to fall apart. So when she met Lucy, it was as though the universe had finally sent her a person who could be her equal. Lucy was charming, confident, and effortless in a way Emma had always admired. Their connection was instant, and for the first time in a long while, Emma felt seen, understood, loved.

In the beginning, it was perfect. Lucy listened when Emma spoke about her childhood, her dreams, her insecurities. She praised Emma for her achievements and comforted her in moments of doubt. They built a life together—weekends spent exploring new cities, evenings filled with laughter, and quiet nights where the world felt far away. Emma's friends and family loved Lucy. She seemed to fit so easily into Emma's world, and Emma, in turn, did everything she could to fit into Lucy's. She had never felt so right with someone.

But slowly, Lucy began to make subtle comments about the people Emma cared about. "Are you sure Sarah really has your best interests at heart?" Lucy would ask, her voice sweet but tinged with doubt. "She's always been a little self-absorbed, don't you think?"

Emma, confused but trusting, would brush it off. "Sarah's my best friend. She's just busy with work."

But Lucy's words lingered, taking root in Emma's mind. She began to notice things—small, seemingly inconsequential moments that added up. When Sarah invited Emma out for coffee, Lucy would feign a look of concern. "I'm sure Sarah's a great friend, but do you really need to spend time with her? I just don't want to see you hurt."

It wasn't just Sarah. Slowly, Lucy started to plant seeds of doubt about everyone in Emma's life. Her family, her co-workers, even her casual friends—Lucy seemed to have an opinion on all of them, an opinion that always cast doubt on their intentions. "Your parents just don't get it," Lucy would say. "They don't really understand you the way I do."

Emma tried to dismiss the feeling that something was off. She had known these people for years. She had built her life around them. But the more time passed, the more isolated she became. At first, it was subtle. The occasional comment, a well-meaning suggestion to "spend more time together" instead of with others. But soon, it became more forceful.

Emma started to second-guess herself. She would think back to conversations she'd had with her friends and family, only to wonder if she had misinterpreted things. Were they really as supportive as they seemed? Had she been too busy with her own life to notice that they didn't actually care? The questions gnawed at her, but Emma couldn't shake them.

One evening, after another quiet dinner with Lucy, Emma decided to call her mother. She hadn't spoken to her in days, and she wanted to make sure everything was okay. But as soon as she picked up the phone, Lucy's voice broke through the silence, soft but firm. "Don't call her now, Emma. You've been talking to her so much lately. Don't you think she's a little too dependent on you?"

Emma froze. "What do you mean?"

Lucy's eyes were filled with something that could have been concern, but there was an edge to it that Emma couldn't quite place. "You've been putting so much energy into everyone else lately. You should focus on us. We're all you need."

The words hit Emma like a slap. She was torn—she hadn't seen her mother in weeks, and yet the thought of calling her felt wrong, somehow. It wasn't like her to doubt herself. It wasn't like her to feel torn between the people she loved and the person she was supposed to be with.

But Lucy had a way of making everything seem so simple. Every decision, every doubt, was always framed as an issue of loyalty. "I'm just worried about you, Emma. I don't want you to get hurt. I know they don't mean to hurt you, but sometimes the people around us just don't know what's best."

In the end, Emma would cancel the call. She'd tell herself that Lucy was right—that her mother, her friends, everyone around her had their own lives and didn't really need her. It was easier this way. It was easier to believe that Lucy was the one who truly understood her.

Time passed, and the isolation deepened. Emma's world began to shrink. She saw her friends less, spoke to her family less, and focused more on being the perfect partner to Lucy. But every time she tried to reach out, every time she questioned Lucy's influence, Lucy would remind her of all the ways her relationships had hurt her in the past.

"Sarah's always so self-centered," Lucy would say, "She's never been there for you when you've really needed her. And your parents—don't even get me started. They don't see you the way I do."

Emma felt like she was drowning in a sea of doubt, but every time she tried to leave, every time she tried to stand up for herself, Lucy would play the perfect victim. She would cry, beg Emma to stay, remind her that no one else cared as much as she did. "I need you, Emma. I'm nothing without you."

And Emma, feeling trapped in a whirlwind of guilt and confusion, would stay. She had been convinced. She had been convinced that Lucy was the only person who truly cared, that she was the one person who could protect her from the cruelty of the world.

But then one day, it all came crashing down. Emma ran into Sarah at the grocery store, and the conversation, though awkward, wasn't what Emma had expected. "I've been trying to reach you for weeks, Em. You've been distant. I know things haven't been easy, but I'm here for you. I always have been."

And for the first time in months, Emma realized the truth. Sarah wasn't the one who had pulled away. It had been her—pulled away by Lucy's manipulations, by her constant undermining of the relationships that had once meant everything to her. In that moment, Emma saw the truth clearly: Lucy had orchestrated everything. Every subtle shift, every planted doubt, every tear had been a tool to control her.

Emma returned home that night, her mind reeling. She knew she needed to make a choice. But when she stepped through the door, Lucy was waiting for her, sitting on the couch, her eyes soft with an unsettling familiarity.

"You've been spending time with Sarah," Lucy said, her voice barely above a whisper, but the threat was clear. "I think it's time for you to choose. Me or her."

In that moment, Emma realized with a sickening clarity that she had already been chosen. The life she had been living, the life Lucy had built around her, had never been hers to begin with. She had been a puppet, manipulated into believing that Lucy's love was the only love worth having. And now, as the walls closed in around her, Emma realized that the price of that love was her own soul.

And she had paid it willingly.

The Ties That Bind

When Mia first met Sophie, she was drawn in by Sophie's vulnerability, the kind of vulnerability that begged to be protected. Sophie's quiet demeanor, the way her eyes seemed to hold a sadness that Mia wanted to erase, made her feel needed in a way no one else had. Sophie was fragile, beautiful, and troubled, and Mia, always the caretaker, promised herself she would make Sophie feel safe. She would be the one to lift Sophie from her despair.

At first, it was a slow and careful dance, the way Sophie allowed Mia to take charge, to guide her, to be the one who solved her problems. They would spend nights talking, with Sophie sharing her childhood trauma, her struggles with anxiety, and her fears about the future. Mia listened, reassured her, and in return, Sophie seemed to fall deeper into her arms, relying on Mia for everything. It was a bond built on need, a need that Mia thought she could handle.

But as the months passed, the cracks began to show. Sophie's emotional dependence grew, and so did her demands. It wasn't just about comforting her anymore; it was about control. Every decision seemed to require Mia's approval. Sophie didn't want Mia to go out with her friends, didn't want her to work late, didn't want her to even spend time alone. "You're always busy, Mia," she'd say, her voice trembling with insecurity. "I just need you here with me. What if something happens and you're not around? What if I'm alone?"

Mia dismissed it at first, thinking it was just the anxiety talking. Sophie had been through so much, after all. She was just asking for support, right? But the requests became more demanding, more frequent. Sophie began to manipulate Mia's time, her social life, and eventually, her mind. "I don't know how I can live without you, Mia. You're the only one who really understands me. If you leave, I... I don't know what I'll do."

At first, Mia took these threats lightly. She would reassure Sophie, tell her that she wasn't going anywhere. But slowly, Mia started to notice how often the threats came. Every time Mia spoke about doing something that didn't involve Sophie—going for a walk alone, meeting a friend, working late—Sophie would become more withdrawn, her voice tinged with something darker. "I just don't think I can be here if you leave me. I don't think I can survive."

Mia laughed it off at first, but the laughter didn't quite reach her eyes. Sophie's words began to burrow into her mind. She started to question whether it was really about love, or whether it was something more insidious. But the more Mia tried to pull away, the more Sophie would draw her in with promises of needing her, of not being able to live without her.

One night, as Mia came home late from work, she found Sophie sitting in the dark. Her face was pale, her body hunched over, her fingers trembling. Mia immediately rushed to her side. "What's wrong? What happened?"

Sophie's voice cracked as she looked up, her eyes filled with a mix of terror and accusation. "You don't love me anymore. I can't do this anymore, Mia. You don't care about me. You've been gone for so long. I just can't handle it. I just can't live with myself if you leave me."

Mia's heart raced, her stomach sinking. "What are you talking about? Sophie, I'm right here. I haven't gone anywhere. I'm not leaving you."

But Sophie wasn't listening. She stood up, her movements shaky, and walked to the bathroom. Mia followed, confused and desperate to understand. Sophie had locked herself in. "Sophie, please open the door. You're scaring me," Mia said, knocking softly. There was no response, only silence.

Then, the sound of something hitting the floor—shattering glass. Mia's heart stopped. "Sophie?" she called, panic creeping into her voice. "Sophie, please."

Sophie opened the door slowly, holding a shattered glass in her hand, the blood from her palm dripping onto the floor. Mia's breath caught in her throat. "I'm sorry," Sophie whispered. "I didn't mean to scare you, but I just... I don't know what else to do. If you leave me, I'll just fall apart. Please don't leave me."

Mia rushed to her side, pressing a towel against Sophie's hand, but Sophie continued to cry, clutching at Mia. "I can't live without you, Mia. I don't want to. I just... I don't know how."

Mia's heart shattered at the sight. She wanted to help, wanted to take away the pain, but the weight of the situation was crushing her. She was being trapped in a cycle, one where she couldn't breathe, couldn't move, couldn't escape. Every time she thought she could pull away, Sophie would pull her back in with promises of needing her, of not surviving without her.

The weeks went by, and the cycle continued. Sophie's emotional demands increased, and Mia found herself growing more and more drained, more isolated from the world she once knew. She stopped calling her friends, stopped visiting her family, stopped doing anything for herself. Every decision, every moment of freedom was met with Sophie's fragile accusations, her constant pleading. "Please don't leave me, Mia. Please, I can't live with the thought of you walking out the door."

Mia started to feel like a prisoner in her own life. She had given up so much—her independence, her happiness, even her sense of self—to keep Sophie from falling apart. But no matter how much she gave, it was never enough. Sophie's demands, her needs, her cries—nothing ever seemed to satisfy her.

And then, one night, as Mia sat on the edge of the bed, her eyes heavy with exhaustion, Sophie looked at her with those same desperate eyes. "You're so tired. You're so worn out, and it's all my fault. But if you leave, I'll have nothing left. I'll die, Mia. I'll die without you."

Mia closed her eyes, her chest tightening. She had heard these words so many times, but each time, they sank deeper into her soul. She didn't know how to escape, didn't know how to break free from the suffocating hold Sophie had on her. She couldn't stand the thought of losing her, of abandoning her, even though she knew that staying meant losing herself entirely.

And so, Mia stayed. She stayed because she couldn't bear the thought of Sophie hurting herself, because she couldn't bear the weight of that guilt. She stayed because, in the end, Sophie had convinced her that she was the only thing that mattered, the only thing that was worth holding on to.

But deep down, Mia knew something darker—she had already lost herself.

Only Me

It started innocently enough, or at least that's how Clara saw it. When she first met Kate, she was drawn to her soft smile, her gentle laugh, the way she seemed to always listen and understand without judgment. Clara had always been someone who craved attention, who needed to feel wanted, and when Kate looked at her with that unspoken understanding, it felt like something she'd been searching for her entire life.

Their relationship moved quickly. Within a few weeks, they were inseparable, spending every moment together. Clara loved it. She had never felt so cherished, so adored. Every text, every phone call, every time Kate reached out, made her feel like she was the center of someone else's world. And for once, it felt good to be wanted like that. But then the requests started. Small at first. A phone call when Clara was out with friends. A text that read, *Where are you?* followed by a quick follow-up, *I miss you, come home soon.*

At first, Clara dismissed it. She knew Kate had a lot of emotional baggage, and her clinginess was just part of her character. She could deal with it. But the demands kept growing. Soon, Clara couldn't make plans without Kate needing to be included or, worse, needing reassurance that she was still important. "Are you sure you still want me around? Sometimes I feel like I'm just a burden," Kate would say, her voice laced with quiet insecurity.

Clara, wanting to be supportive, would reassure her. "You're not a burden, Kate. I love you. I want you around. It's just that I need some space sometimes." But when she said that, Kate would pull away, her eyes filling with hurt. And Clara, feeling the guilt wash over her, would apologize, swear that it wasn't about Kate, that it was just her needing a little time to herself.

But the truth was, it wasn't just the occasional call or text that began to weigh on her. It was how quickly Kate turned every situation into an emotional crisis. Clara found herself walking on eggshells, careful not to upset Kate, afraid that any small mistake would send her into a spiral of doubt. Every time she spoke to a friend or spent time away, Kate would react as though it was a betrayal, as though no one else could possibly care for her the way Clara did. "I don't understand why you need them, Clara," Kate would say softly, her voice trembling with quiet desperation. "I don't get why they mean more to you than I do. Why can't it just be us?"

And that was the problem. Over time, it became *just* them. Clara started canceling plans with her friends, avoiding family gatherings, all because Kate made her feel like those people were a threat to their relationship. She started to believe Kate's words: *They don't care about you the way I do.* In Kate's world, love was a suffocating thing, a thing that couldn't exist without constant reassurance and constant attention. Kate made Clara feel that without her, she would be lost, as though her life would have no meaning. Every moment spent apart felt like a moment of betrayal, even if it was just a phone call with her mother.

"Don't you see?" Kate whispered one night, when Clara tried to explain how overwhelming everything had become. "I'm the only one who really loves you. They'll leave you eventually, like everyone else. You can't trust anyone but me."

Clara tried to brush it off, but the doubt began to creep in. Kate was right, wasn't she? No one had ever cared for Clara like this before. No one had ever made her feel as important, as necessary. It was easier to believe that Kate was the only one who truly loved her, that the people around her were just passing figures who would never understand her the way Kate did.

Days turned into weeks, and Clara's world began to shrink. She was losing touch with everyone—her friends, her family, even herself. She had become so consumed by Kate's need for her, by the constant emotional demands, that she could hardly remember what it was like to be happy on her own. Kate had convinced her that her happiness could only exist in the space between them, that Clara's existence was incomplete without her. Every moment alone felt like a betrayal, like a lie.

One evening, as Clara sat on the couch, scrolling through her phone, a message from her best friend Sarah popped up. It had been weeks since they last spoke, and Clara immediately felt a pang of guilt. She had ignored Sarah's calls, never returned her texts. Sarah had been her best friend for years, but now, she felt like a distant memory.

"Clara, I miss you. We need to talk soon. I'm worried about you."

Clara stared at the message, feeling a weight in her chest. It was a reminder of the life she used to have, of the people who once cared for her. But Kate's presence was like a shadow in the corner of her mind, and before she could think, her fingers were already typing. *I can't right now, Sarah. I'm with Kate. I'll call you later.*

As soon as she hit send, Kate walked into the room, her eyes scanning Clara's face. "Who was that?" she asked softly, but there was a hardness beneath the question, a possessiveness that Clara couldn't ignore.

"Just Sarah," Clara replied, her voice shaky. "She just wanted to talk, but I told her I was busy."

Kate's eyes softened, but Clara saw the flicker of satisfaction behind them. She had done the right thing. She had chosen Kate.

But the moment passed quickly. The weight of her own decision settled into Clara's bones, and as Kate wrapped her arms around her, whispering sweet nothings into her ear, Clara felt the crushing realization hit her. This wasn't love. This was control. This wasn't care. This was suffocation.

Days later, when she returned to her phone to see a new message from Sarah, Clara found herself unable to read it. She didn't want to face it. She didn't want to hear the concern in Sarah's voice. It had been too long now, and the space between them had grown too wide. She didn't know if she could fix it. But more than that, she didn't know if she could fix herself.

The lesson had been woven through every moment of their relationship: the lies, the manipulation, the isolation. She had believed she was loved, but in reality, she had been trapped in a lie, caught in a relationship where her worth was measured by her constant availability, her constant submission to Kate's need for control. And the most frightening part was that Clara was starting to believe that this was the only kind of love that existed.

As Kate whispered more reassurances into her ear, Clara realized with sickening clarity: *I don't know if I can live without this.* And as the walls closed in, she understood that in the end, she might never escape.

The Weight of Her Words

Sophie had always been sure of herself—at least, that's how she liked to think. She had been independent, successful in her career, confident in her friendships. But when she met Zoe, everything began to shift. Zoe was different from anyone Sophie had ever known. Charming, quick-witted, and effortlessly confident, Zoe had an aura of authority that drew Sophie in. Sophie found herself intrigued by Zoe's ability to control any situation, to make everyone around her feel like they were just a little bit less. Zoe's presence was magnetic, and Sophie couldn't help but admire her.

At first, it was flattering. Zoe would make Sophie laugh with her dry humor, compliment her looks, and praise her intelligence. Sophie felt like she had found someone who truly saw her. But slowly, the compliments began to feel hollow, like a prelude to something else. Zoe would make little remarks, disguised as jokes, that cut deeper than Sophie realized at the time. "You always overthink everything, Sophie. You're so smart, but sometimes it's like your brain is a prison." Or, "I really love that dress on you, though, it hides your hips well."

Sophie laughed it off, telling herself that Zoe was just teasing, just being playful. But the more time they spent together, the more Zoe's words seemed to linger in the air, like smoke that wouldn't dissipate. Sophie found herself questioning everything she did—every outfit, every word she said, every decision she made. At first, she thought it was just normal self-doubt. After all, Zoe was so confident, so assured of herself. But Sophie couldn't shake the feeling that something wasn't right.

Zoe began to subtly dictate the way Sophie lived her life. "You don't really need to hang out with Sarah anymore, do you? She's always so negative," Zoe said one evening, her voice casual but firm. "It's good for you to spend time with people who actually lift you up."

Sophie hesitated. Sarah had been her best friend for years. But Zoe's words made her feel like Sarah wasn't worth her time, that she was a burden Sophie didn't need. Zoe had a way of making Sophie feel like she was doing something wrong—something unworthy—every time she tried to keep connections outside of their relationship.

Over time, the comments grew more frequent, more cutting. "Why did you buy that? You know you can't afford it," Zoe would say when Sophie bought herself something new. "I don't know why you're still trying so hard at work. You're so much better than the people there. They don't appreciate you."

Sophie began to feel like a shadow of herself. The woman who used to confidently make decisions was replaced by someone who second-guessed everything. What started as playful teasing became constant criticism. Sophie found herself constantly apologizing for things she hadn't done, or things she hadn't meant. "I didn't mean to make you upset," she would say, but Zoe would always respond with a look, a shrug that made Sophie feel smaller, weaker.

The guilt began to eat away at her. She was constantly worried that her actions were wrong, that she wasn't living up to Zoe's expectations. The more Sophie tried to prove herself, the more Zoe pointed out her flaws, her shortcomings. "You're so indecisive. You can't even order food without asking me what you should get," Zoe would remark, her voice dripping with condescension. "It's really tiring, Sophie. I just want you to be sure of yourself for once."

Sophie wanted to be sure of herself, wanted to be the confident woman she once was. But with every passing day, Zoe's words began to feel like they had become her own thoughts. Sophie couldn't make a decision without wondering what Zoe would think. She couldn't go anywhere without wondering if Zoe would approve. She was no longer sure of her own worth.

One evening, after Zoe had made yet another comment about Sophie's inability to make decisions, Sophie felt a growing sense of panic. She couldn't take it anymore. She couldn't think straight. She found herself standing in front of the mirror, staring at her reflection, barely recognizing the person looking back at her. Who was she now? Who was she becoming?

She went to bed that night, too exhausted to cry, but too terrified to sleep. In the morning, she woke up early, hoping to escape the suffocating weight of Zoe's constant presence. She called her mother, her heart racing. "Mom, I don't know what's happening to me," Sophie said, her voice shaking. "I feel like I've lost myself. I don't know how to make decisions anymore. I don't know what's real."

Her mother's voice was filled with concern. "Sophie, you've always been a strong girl. Don't let anyone make you doubt yourself. You're smart, you're capable. You don't need anyone's permission to live your life."

Sophie held the phone tightly, wishing she could feel that strength, wishing she could be the person her mother saw. "But what if I'm wrong? What if I'm just... not good enough?"

The words echoed in her mind long after she hung up the phone. She was constantly measuring herself against Zoe's expectations, unable to trust her own instincts. She began to distance herself from everyone—her friends, her family. Zoe made it clear, every chance she got, that Sophie didn't need anyone but her.

And then, one day, it happened. Zoe looked at Sophie, her expression calm but dangerous. "You're just so weak sometimes," Zoe said, her voice low. "It's exhausting to always have to carry you. You don't even know who you are anymore, do you?"

Sophie's heart dropped. For the first time, the truth hit her like a punch in the stomach. Zoe wasn't in love with her. Zoe didn't want a partner. Zoe wanted a puppet, someone who would do everything she said without question, someone whose every thought and action was determined by Zoe's will.

Sophie stood there, frozen, unable to breathe. She had given so much of herself to Zoe, had allowed her to tear down everything she had once believed about herself. And now, she was nothing. She had become a shell of the woman she used to be, a woman who could no longer trust her own thoughts, her own choices.

"I don't know if I can do this anymore," Sophie whispered, the words slipping out before she could stop them.

Zoe didn't even look surprised. "You can't leave, Sophie," she said, her voice soft, but cold. "You wouldn't know how to live without me. I've made you. You're nothing without me."

Sophie felt the truth of those words sink in, deeper than anything Zoe had ever said. She was nothing. She had become nothing. And as Zoe looked at her with pity, Sophie realized she had become the puppet in Zoe's game. The life she once had, the woman she once was, was gone.

And in that moment, Sophie understood: the one thing she had lost was the ability to choose herself.

The Only One Who Cares

It wasn't love at first sight, but it was something close. Maddie met Elise at a mutual friend's gathering—a quiet, almost withdrawn woman with dark eyes that seemed to understand more than they let on. Elise was beautiful in a subtle way. There was something magnetic about her, a quiet confidence that intrigued Maddie. It was easy to be drawn to her, to feel as though she was the kind of person who could protect you without asking for anything in return.

In the beginning, Elise seemed perfect. She would listen to Maddie's stories with rapt attention, offering gentle advice and the kind of empathy Maddie had never known before. Every time Maddie had a problem, Elise would swoop in, providing solutions, reassurance, and an unwavering belief that they were meant to be. Maddie had never felt so seen, so cared for. Elise made her feel like the center of the universe, and Maddie couldn't help but think that maybe, just maybe, this was what love was supposed to feel like.

But over time, Maddie began to notice small things—small ways Elise started to shape her world. At first, it was nothing more than an offhand comment. "You don't need to hang out with Sarah so much," Elise would say, her tone light, as if she was simply looking out for her. "She's always so negative. I can't stand the way she talks about you."

Maddie didn't want to believe it at first. Sarah was her best friend, someone she'd known for years, someone who had been there for her through thick and thin. But when she looked at it from Elise's point of view, Sarah's words did seem a little harsh sometimes. And Elise, well, Elise always made her feel so good about herself. The more she listened, the more she began to question her loyalty to Sarah.

A few weeks later, it was the same story with her family. "They only care about you when it's convenient for them, Maddie," Elise would say. "You don't need them. They don't really love you the way I do." At first, Maddie tried to resist, tried to defend her family, but the seeds of doubt were already planted. Elise never asked for anything directly; she just subtly made Maddie feel like no one could care for her the way Elise did. No one understood her the way Elise did. No one would ever love her like Elise loved her.

Soon, Maddie found herself drifting away from her family and friends. She started canceling plans, avoiding phone calls, and making excuses to spend more time with Elise. Every moment spent away from her felt like a betrayal, and Elise made sure Maddie knew it. She would pull away, give her the silent treatment, and act distant whenever Maddie wasn't available, making Maddie feel guilty for wanting to maintain any connection outside their relationship. "You know I'm the only one who truly cares about you," Elise would say, her voice soft, almost pleading. "You don't need anyone else. They'll all leave you in the end. Only I will stay. Only I will always love you."

The manipulation was subtle, slow, and Maddie didn't realize how deeply she was sinking into it. She became more isolated, more dependent on Elise's approval, and she started to believe that her life before Elise—her friends, her family, her independence—wasn't as important as Elise's love. The more Elise gave her affection, the more Maddie felt like she couldn't function without it. The more Elise subtly tore down every relationship that existed before her, the more Maddie relied on her, believing that no one else could possibly love her the way Elise did.

One evening, as they sat together in their small apartment, Maddie picked up her phone, scrolling through her messages. She hesitated when she saw a message from Sarah, asking if they could meet up. She hadn't seen Sarah in weeks. A small part of her wanted to see her, wanted to reconnect with the person who had once been so important to her. But when she looked up at Elise, who was sitting beside her, that familiar sense of guilt crept in. Elise hadn't said anything, but there was a shift in her expression, a look that made Maddie feel like she was doing something wrong.

"You're not really going to meet up with her, are you?" Elise asked softly, her voice steady, but there was an undercurrent of something darker. "You know she doesn't understand you like I do. She's just going to pull you away from me again."

Maddie felt her heart race. The tension in the room thickened as she put the phone down, her hands suddenly cold. She wanted to go see Sarah, but something in Elise's eyes, something in the way she spoke, made Maddie feel like she would be betraying her—betraying the one person who had made her feel truly loved.

"I don't know," Maddie said quietly, her voice barely above a whisper. "I just thought it would be nice to catch up."

Elise leaned in, her hand resting on Maddie's knee, her touch gentle, but her grip firm. "I'm the only one who really cares about you. I've always been the one to pick you up when you're down. She doesn't do that for you, Maddie. You can't see it now, but she'll always let you down in the end."

Maddie's mind felt foggy. The words echoed in her head, drowning out everything else. Was Elise right? Was Sarah really just a distraction? Maddie looked down at her phone, and then back at Elise, who smiled softly, her eyes filled with affection.

"I just don't want to lose you," Elise said. "I'm all you have, Maddie. You need me."

And in that moment, Maddie knew what she had to do. She turned off her phone, set it aside, and nodded at Elise. "You're right," she whispered, though the words tasted like ash in her mouth. "I don't need anyone else."

Elise's smile grew, and she wrapped her arms around Maddie, holding her tightly. "I knew you would understand," she said, her voice sweet and filled with satisfaction.

But as Maddie leaned into her arms, something inside her flickered, a tiny voice in the back of her mind whispering that something was terribly wrong. She couldn't quite grasp it, but she felt it—the way her life was shrinking, the way her world had become smaller and smaller with every choice she made to stay with Elise.

As the days passed, Maddie grew more and more suffocated. Elise's love, once something that felt like a lifeline, was now the only thing that held her in place. The truth was clear now, though she couldn't fully admit it: she had lost herself, piece by piece, until there was nothing left but the reflection of Elise's desires. And she knew, deep down, that the more she gave, the less she would ever be able to leave.

Elise had made sure of that.

The Wedge Between Us

Lena never thought she would find someone like Katie. The moment they met, something clicked. Katie was different from the others—there was a quiet intensity about her, a way of making Lena feel like the most important person in the room. She was confident, beautiful, and captivating in a way that made Lena feel safe, seen, and valued. For the first time in a long while, Lena felt like she wasn't invisible. Katie made her believe that she deserved to be loved, that she was worthy of someone's devotion.

In the beginning, it was perfect. Katie was affectionate, showering Lena with attention and care. They spent long hours talking, sharing their dreams and fears. Katie always seemed to know exactly what Lena needed. But after a few months, small cracks began to form in their relationship, unnoticed at first, but growing slowly, silently. Katie would comment on Lena's friendships, the people in her life, in subtle ways.

"Are you sure you want to hang out with Sarah again? You know she's always so self-absorbed," Katie would say one night, casually picking at her food, eyes fixed on the table.

Lena frowned, taken aback. "What do you mean? She's one of my oldest friends. You know how close we are."

Katie would smile softly, the tone of her voice softening. "I'm not saying she's a bad person, but she doesn't treat you the way I do. She's always about herself. I just want you to think about it, Lena. You deserve to be with people who really see you."

Lena would brush it off, but the seed of doubt had been planted. Over the next few weeks, Katie's comments became more frequent. "You know, I've noticed how much time you spend on the phone with your parents," Katie said one evening, her voice filled with concern. "I get it, they're family. But it's like you don't need me as much when you're with them. You should be spending more time here, with me. Don't you want to be with someone who makes you feel special, who's here for you, always?"

Lena felt the uncomfortable shift. Her parents were important to her, but something in Katie's voice made her second-guess her priorities. After all, she *was* with Katie now, wasn't she? But it didn't stop there. Katie began to isolate Lena more and more. Every time Lena made plans with anyone, Katie would find a reason to be upset, to create tension. She would make quiet accusations, like how Lena wasn't truly there for her, how her friends and family would eventually abandon her, leaving her with nothing but Katie.

At first, Lena was resistant. She knew she couldn't cut people out of her life. She'd always been close to her friends and family, and she wasn't ready to give them up. But as time went on, Katie's manipulations became more subtle, more insidious. When Lena tried to meet Sarah for coffee, Katie would sulk, telling Lena she didn't care about her. When Lena went to visit her parents, Katie would accuse her of loving them more than her.

"You don't understand," Katie would say, her voice a mix of hurt and anger. "I need you. I want to be the most important person in your life. You don't need anyone else. They'll just take you away from me, and I'll be left alone."

Lena would apologize, as she always did, telling herself it was just the pressure Katie felt, the jealousy that came from loving her so much. But slowly, it wore her down. Lena started second-guessing herself, questioning her relationships. Were Sarah and her family really as supportive as they claimed? Or was Katie right? Was she just trying to cling to people who didn't really have her best interests at heart?

The last straw came one night when Lena tried to go out with a group of friends. Katie had been quiet all day, distant, her mood shifting in ways Lena didn't understand. As Lena was getting ready to leave, Katie's voice broke through the silence.

"You're really going out with them tonight?" Katie asked, her voice laced with something Lena couldn't quite place.

Lena hesitated, her hand hovering over the door. "I just wanted to catch up with everyone. You know, it's been a while."

Katie's eyes narrowed, her face pale. "You know I hate it when you leave me for them. Don't you realize what you're doing? You're pushing me away. You're abandoning me."

Lena tried to explain, tried to reassure Katie that it wasn't like that, but Katie wouldn't listen. She crossed her arms, her expression cold and hurt. "If you leave, don't bother coming back. I don't need people who don't need me. I can't be with someone who doesn't choose me."

The words cut deeper than Lena wanted to admit. For the first time, she felt a sickening sense of dread. Katie's demands, her jealousy, had crossed a line. But when Lena opened her mouth to protest, to tell Katie she needed space, Katie's expression softened, and she whispered, "You know you'll regret it if you go, don't you? I'm the only one who truly cares about you. The only one who will never hurt you. Don't you trust me?"

Lena's heart pounded in her chest. Katie's words, spoken so softly, so convincingly, had worked their way under her skin. She couldn't bear the thought of losing her. And in that moment, she didn't even want to.

"I'm sorry," Lena whispered, stepping back into the apartment. Katie's arms wrapped around her immediately, holding her tight, her grip possessive and warm.

Lena stayed in for the night, ignoring her friends' messages, letting the feeling of suffocation settle in. She didn't want to fight anymore, didn't want to push Katie away. Slowly, everything outside their relationship—the people, the places, the life she had before Katie—began to fade. And the more she tried to convince herself that she was doing what was right, the more the guilt built inside her.

As the weeks went by, Lena found herself more isolated, more dependent on Katie's approval. The relationship with her friends, with her family—everything became strained, distant. And each time she tried to reach out, Katie's voice, that cold, dangerous tone, would echo in her mind, reminding her of her worthlessness without Katie.

But when Lena looked in the mirror one night, the realization hit her with a sickening force: she didn't know who she was anymore. She had let Katie destroy everything, let her isolate her from the people who had once loved her. She had built a life based on fear—fear of being alone, fear of losing Katie, fear of not being enough.

And in that moment, Lena understood that the true loss was not the distance between her and her family—it was the distance she had created from herself.

Unraveled

Emma had always considered herself a rational person. She kept a tight grip on her emotions, made careful decisions, and looked for evidence before she drew conclusions. That's why, when she met Natalie, everything felt so different. Natalie was spontaneous, passionate, and free-spirited. Emma was captivated by her energy, the way she made everything seem so alive. It didn't take long before Emma was completely enamored, convinced that this was the kind of love that could change her life forever.

In the beginning, everything seemed perfect. They laughed together, spent late nights talking about their dreams, and shared moments of quiet joy. Emma felt alive in a way she never had before. Natalie made her feel wanted, special, and in a way, understood. It felt like they were building something real, something that no one could take away.

But soon, the cracks started to appear. It began with small, almost dismissible comments. Natalie would brush off their shared memories, claiming they didn't happen the way Emma remembered. "You're so dramatic, Em," she would say, her voice laced with amusement. "That's not how it happened at all. We never really had that much fun, did we? Don't you remember how awkward it was?"

At first, Emma laughed it off. It wasn't possible that Natalie had forgotten their happiest moments together. They had spent hours talking about their future, the trips they'd take, the life they'd build. But over time, the comments became more frequent. "I don't know why you're so nostalgic about that trip," Natalie would say one night, a strange coldness in her tone. "It was a disaster, Em. We fought the whole time. You really think it was fun?"

Emma's chest tightened at the mention of the trip, which she had always seen as a milestone in their relationship. It had been one of the happiest times of her life, filled with laughter, shared discoveries, and moments of intimacy. But Natalie was right in a way, wasn't she? They had fought a few times during the trip, had differences, had their moments of stress. Maybe Emma had been idealizing it, turning it into something more than it had been.

But then, the memories began to fade. The laughter seemed less genuine in retrospect, the moments of connection more fleeting. Every time Emma tried to bring up a happy memory, Natalie would find a way to twist it, to make it feel insignificant. "It's all in your head, Em," she'd say softly, as if she were soothing a child. "We never had a perfect relationship. You've always been too idealistic. It was just another trip. It wasn't as great as you think."

Emma's doubt began to eat away at her. She had always trusted her memory, her ability to hold onto the good moments, the important things. But now, she started to question everything. Were those memories real? Had she imagined the moments of happiness? Was Natalie right—had their entire relationship been nothing more than a series of mundane, forgettable moments? Emma felt like she was losing control of her thoughts.

It wasn't just the memories. The way Natalie spoke to her, the way she dismissed Emma's concerns, started to make Emma question her own perceptions. "You're overreacting," Natalie would say whenever Emma expressed discomfort with something, whether it was a casual remark, a gesture, or an argument they'd had. "I don't know why you're so upset. You always blow things out of proportion."

Emma tried to hold onto herself, tried to remember who she was before Natalie. But the more Natalie fed her doubts, the more her sense of self began to slip away. She found herself questioning the simplest things: her own thoughts, her own actions, her own intentions. It wasn't just the past that Natalie manipulated—it was Emma's very identity. "You've always been insecure, haven't you?" Natalie would say one night, her voice gentle, almost caring. "You're not as strong as you think. You've never been able to handle things the way you think you have."

Emma felt a growing sense of panic, as though the ground beneath her was slipping away. Was Natalie right? Had she always been weak? Was she truly as unreliable as Natalie made her feel? Every time Emma thought she had a grasp on reality, Natalie would tear it down, piece by piece.

The breaking point came on their anniversary. Emma had planned a special evening—dinner at their favorite restaurant, followed by a walk under the stars. It was a celebration of the time they had spent together, of the love they had shared. But when they arrived at the restaurant, something was different. Natalie was distant, cold. The spark that had once made their relationship feel alive seemed to have vanished.

Emma tried to engage, tried to remind Natalie of the happy moments they had shared, but Natalie was unresponsive, offering nothing but terse replies. After dinner, they walked to a nearby park. The quiet between them was thick, suffocating. Emma could feel the weight of their past, the years of love and connection, slipping away with every step.

Finally, as they reached a bench, Emma couldn't take it anymore. "What's happening, Natalie? Why are you so distant tonight? We've always been able to talk about things, but now... now it's like you don't even care."

Natalie looked at her with a mixture of indifference and pity. "You're imagining things, Em. We've never had that perfect love you keep trying to hold onto. You keep thinking everything was better than it was. You really think I've been as invested in this as you have? I've been trying to get you to see that. But you just can't let go of the fantasy."

The words hit Emma like a slap. For the first time, she realized what had been happening all along. Natalie hadn't just been twisting their memories; she had been erasing them, reshaping them into something that fit her narrative. Natalie didn't want Emma to remember the good times. She wanted her to feel alone, unworthy, dependent on Natalie's love, and unable to make sense of her own life without it.

Emma sat on the bench, her heart heavy, her mind spinning with the realization. She had spent so long believing in a love that didn't exist—not in the way she thought. And now, it was clear. Natalie wasn't just manipulating her memories. She was manipulating her very sense of self.

As the night stretched on, Emma understood with chilling clarity that she had lost herself in the relationship, had let Natalie take control of every thought, every memory. She had let Natalie rewrite her history, and in doing so, she had erased her own truth.

And as the realization settled in, Emma felt the last threads of her identity slip away—gone forever in the darkness of Natalie's gaslighting.

The Price of Love

When Sara met Olivia, it felt like destiny. Olivia had an energy about her that was magnetic—charming, confident, and unshakably kind. She had this way of making everyone feel special, and Sara, for the first time in a long while, felt like she mattered. Olivia's attention was like a lifeline, pulling Sara from the depths of loneliness she had been drowning in. Every smile, every thoughtful gesture, made Sara feel seen, valued—worthy of love.

The first few months were filled with excitement and affection. They would spend days wrapped in each other's presence, sharing late-night conversations, spontaneous trips, and endless laughter. Olivia would show Sara how to be present in the moment, how to enjoy life more fully. "You work too hard," Olivia would say, her voice soft, almost concerned. "You deserve to relax, to enjoy the little things. I want to take care of you, Sara."

It felt good to be taken care of, to have someone who made her feel cherished. Olivia would surprise her with little gifts, thoughtful notes, and acts of kindness. At first, it felt natural—Sara never expected anything in return. But over time, things began to shift.

"Here, I made you dinner," Olivia would say one evening, setting down a plate. "You've been working so much. You owe it to yourself to take a break."

Sara would smile, grateful, but the words "owe it to yourself" hung in the air. She didn't think much of it at first, but slowly, it started to feel like Olivia was keeping track of every kindness, every favor.

As weeks went by, Olivia would remind Sara of all the things she had done for her. "Remember when I took care of you when you were sick?" Olivia would say, her tone casual but with an edge of something else. "You're so lucky I'm here, taking care of everything. You know, not everyone would do that for you. I don't think anyone else cares about you the way I do."

Sara's chest tightened when Olivia said things like this. She had never thought about it that way. She had always believed that helping each other was just part of a healthy relationship. But now, she was starting to feel the weight of Olivia's words. With every favor, every act of kindness, it felt as though there was an unspoken transaction happening between them.

"Thank you for helping me with the laundry," Olivia said one night as Sara folded clothes. "I'm not sure what I would do without you. You're so good to me. You know, I don't think anyone would ever put in the effort you do. You really owe it to me, Sara. I'm the one who makes sure you're happy."

Sara's heart sank. "I never expected anything in return," she said, trying to reassure herself. "I just want to help. You don't have to keep track of everything."

But Olivia's smile was almost too sweet. "I know you don't expect anything. But you really should be grateful. You know, I've been there for you in ways no one else would. Don't you think you owe me something for all that I've done for you?"

Sara felt the confusion growing inside her. She hadn't realized it before, but the more she gave, the more Olivia seemed to demand in return. Every act of kindness, every gesture of love, became something that Sara had to repay. And it wasn't just little things anymore. It was everything. Olivia started to expect more, to point out that Sara should do more in return for all she had "sacrificed" for her.

One night, after a long day at work, Sara was exhausted. She collapsed on the couch, hoping to relax for a few minutes. Olivia sat down beside her, brushing her hair back gently. "You've had a long day," she said softly. "I really wish you could be more mindful. You know, if you took better care of yourself, I wouldn't have to keep doing everything for you. I'm the one who's been keeping us afloat."

Sara felt the guilt well up inside her, as it always did. "I don't mean to burden you," she whispered, looking away, not able to meet Olivia's gaze.

Olivia's eyes softened, but there was a coldness behind her smile. "It's okay, sweetie. I just want you to realize how much I've done for you. I've always been the one who's been there when you needed someone. You know, not everyone would do what I've done. And I don't mind taking care of you. But you have to understand, you can't keep taking from me without giving something back. I need you to remember that."

The words echoed in Sara's mind long after Olivia had gone to bed. The idea that she owed Olivia for every act of kindness was like a weight she couldn't escape. She couldn't relax without feeling guilty, couldn't enjoy the affection without wondering what she had to give in return. The joy in their relationship had turned into a ledger, with Olivia keeping track of every favor, every gesture, every ounce of love Sara gave her.

It was only when Sara tried to leave for a weekend with friends that she realized just how much Olivia had manipulated her. Olivia's reaction was swift and intense.

"Why are you going without me?" Olivia demanded, her voice low, but laced with something Sara hadn't heard before—something that sent a chill through her. "Do you think anyone else is going to care for you the way I do? They won't appreciate you. They won't love you like I do. You owe me, Sara. You really do."

Sara's heart raced, her hands trembling as she packed. "I'm just spending time with my friends," she said, her voice barely above a whisper, "I need space, Olivia. I need time to myself."

Olivia stepped closer, her face soft, her voice quiet. "I'm the only one who really understands you, Sara. You can't leave me. You owe me everything, and if you go, I'll be alone. No one else will ever love you like I do."

The suffocating reality hit Sara like a ton of bricks. She felt trapped, cornered by the woman she loved. Every act of kindness, every gesture of affection, had become a debt that Sara couldn't pay. The love she had once felt had been twisted into something dark, something that chained her to Olivia in ways she hadn't realized until it was too late.

As Sara stood there, her mind swirling with the guilt of leaving, the suffocating weight of Olivia's words, she knew she was caught. She was no longer a partner in a relationship of mutual care. She was a debtor, and Olivia was the creditor, always reminding her of the price she would never be able to repay.

And so, when she put the suitcase down and agreed to stay, she knew the real cost. She had lost herself. She had lost her right to choose. And in that dark silence, she understood: the more she gave, the more Olivia took, until there was nothing left of Sara but a shell, trapped in a love that demanded everything.

The Walls Between Us

When Claire met Rose, she never imagined how quickly things would change. Rose was magnetic, with a warmth that made Claire feel seen in a way she hadn't known she was missing. Their connection was instant—Rose listened like she cared, smiled like she meant it, and made Claire feel like the center of her world. It was everything Claire had always wanted. It felt like they had an unspoken bond, something rare, special, and worth holding onto.

At first, it was subtle—the way Rose would suggest little things, always framed as requests. "Would you mind if we spent tonight in? I just want to relax with you," Rose would say, her voice soft and inviting. Claire, happy to oblige, agreed. It felt good to give Rose what she needed. It was just one night, after all, one small change in their routine.

But over time, it wasn't just one night. It became a regular occurrence. Rose would suggest they stay in more often, avoid going out with Claire's friends, and, at first, Claire didn't mind. She enjoyed Rose's company and had always preferred quiet nights over crowded gatherings. "I'm just tired of going out all the time," Rose explained one evening. "We don't need anyone else. I just want to be with you."

Claire, reassured by the gentle tone, agreed without question. But slowly, she began to notice that their outings, even with family, were becoming less frequent. Rose would ask her to cancel plans, to call in sick to work when it seemed unnecessary, to stay home when Claire thought she needed to get out. The requests seemed harmless at first, and when Claire hesitated, Rose would convince her with soft persuasion, "We don't need to be around other people. Don't you want to spend this time with me? I feel better when it's just us."

Eventually, Claire stopped making plans without Rose. She didn't question it—Rose had become the center of her life. She started to give up things she used to enjoy. Dinners with friends became rare. Work events, even professional networking opportunities, were canceled in favor of spending time with Rose. Every time Claire thought about doing something independently, she found herself feeling guilty. Rose's sweet, needy smile would come to her mind, and Claire couldn't bear the thought of letting her down.

One day, Claire mentioned meeting her mother for coffee. Rose's face tightened ever so slightly, and when Claire noticed, she quickly backpedaled, "I'll go another time. I'm sure Mom won't mind." Rose's smile was warm, but Claire could feel the shift, the subtle tension in the air. "You don't need to spend time with her, though. You know I'm the one who really understands you, right?" Rose said, voice low and coaxing. "You don't need them. You have me. I'm the only one who matters."

Claire felt a lump form in her throat. She hadn't realized how much Rose had subtly eroded her relationships with those she loved. It wasn't a sudden shift; it was gradual, the way someone waters a plant, day by day. One request, one slight shift in routine, one change after another, until the old life Claire had built was nothing but an echo.

When Claire mentioned meeting Sarah, her oldest friend, for a catch-up, Rose's response was different. "I don't like the way she talks about you sometimes. She's always so critical. Don't you think she's a little too... harsh?" Rose asked, her tone casual but with an undercurrent of concern. "I just want you to be happy. I don't want you to feel like you have to put up with her."

Claire hesitated. "She's been my friend for years, Rose. I don't think she's harsh. She just... wants the best for me."

"I'm the best for you, Claire," Rose responded, her eyes intense, her voice low. "You don't need anyone else. You can always count on me. I don't want you to feel like you have to prove something to them. They won't be there for you the way I am."

Claire sat back, her mind in a fog. Rose had a way of twisting things, of making her feel like she wasn't doing enough, like every action had to be measured by Rose's standards. It was draining, but it felt normal now, like something she had always known—always accepted. She began to notice that every time she tried to step away, even for a moment, Rose's requests would feel more urgent, more pressing.

A few months later, Claire's anxiety grew. She wasn't sure when it had happened, but she realized that she had stopped making decisions for herself. Everything, from what she ate to where she went, had started to revolve around Rose's needs, Rose's comfort. And when Claire did make a choice that didn't align with what Rose wanted, she felt the cold distance between them, the subtle resentment simmering beneath Rose's surface.

One night, after a long silence, Claire tried to voice her concerns. "I feel like... I feel like I've been losing touch with everything. I haven't seen my friends in months. I haven't even spent time with my mom. I'm starting to feel like I'm losing myself."

Rose's expression softened, her hand gently taking Claire's. "You haven't lost yourself, sweetie. You're just focusing on what matters. I know you want to be there for everyone, but they don't need you the way I do. You don't need anyone else. You're everything I want. I've given you everything, and you know I'd do anything for you. I just need you to be with me, to be here with me. No one else will care for you the way I do. I'm all you need."

Claire's chest tightened. She felt a heavy, suffocating weight on her chest. The reality of the words, the control, hit her all at once. It wasn't love. It was manipulation, a slow erosion of her independence, her identity. Every step she had taken to please Rose had been a step away from herself.

But when Claire tried to leave, to take back some part of her life, she found that Rose had already woven her life into every fabric of Claire's existence. The thought of walking away—of leaving Rose—was met with a paralyzing fear, a doubt that she couldn't shake. How would she even begin to function without Rose?

That night, Claire stayed. Rose's hands were warm and gentle around her, but all Claire could feel was the weight of the cage she had unknowingly stepped into. She had given up everything—her independence, her friends, her family—and for what? A love that demanded everything, that gave nothing but control.

And deep down, Claire knew that leaving now, walking away from the life she had built with Rose, would be the hardest thing she would ever do. It wasn't love she was running from. It was the slow, escalating control that had locked her in, and now, it was the only thing she knew.

The walls had closed in, and Claire was too far gone to see a way out.

The Thin Line Between Love and Control

Megan had always been the quiet one. Shy, introspective, and careful with her words, she'd spent years feeling invisible to most of the world. That was until she met Eliza. Eliza was everything Megan wasn't—bold, confident, and full of life. She seemed to light up every room she walked into, commanding attention without trying. Megan found herself drawn to Eliza immediately, captivated by the way she moved through life with ease and certainty. Eliza made her feel noticed in a way she never had before, and Megan quickly fell under her spell.

In the beginning, their relationship was intoxicating. Eliza would constantly reassure Megan that she was special, telling her that there was no one else like her. "You're the only one who really gets me," Eliza would whisper, her fingers trailing gently along Megan's arm. Megan basked in the warmth of her affection, eager to be everything Eliza needed. For a while, it felt like the most natural thing in the world. Megan had never felt so loved, so cared for.

But as time went on, Megan began to notice small things—slight shifts in Eliza's behavior that made her uneasy. Eliza would often bring up other women Megan knew, sometimes friends, sometimes acquaintances, and the tone of her voice would shift. "You seem to spend a lot of time talking to Sarah lately," Eliza would comment, her voice light but sharp. "Does she make you feel good about yourself? Do you need her approval more than mine?"

At first, Megan brushed it off. It was just a passing comment, she thought. Eliza was just being protective, wanting to keep their bond strong. But the comments kept coming. "I saw you laughing with Emma yesterday. You really seem to enjoy her company," Eliza said one night, as they sat on the couch together. "I can't help but wonder if you feel closer to her than you do to me. Am I just not enough for you?"

Megan felt a knot tighten in her stomach. She hadn't done anything wrong, had she? She tried to reassure Eliza, telling her that Emma was just a friend, that nothing had changed between them. But Eliza would never seem convinced. Every time Megan interacted with someone outside of their relationship, Eliza's jealousy would flare up, and Megan would feel like she had to explain herself. The words would always come out softer, apologetic. "It's just a friend," Megan would say, "I'm not trying to hurt you." But deep down, she was starting to wonder whether there was a truth to Eliza's suspicions.

Then one night, things took a turn. Megan had planned a dinner with her colleagues, a chance to celebrate the success of a project at work. Eliza didn't take it well. "You're going out again?" she asked, her voice quiet but edged with something darker. "Don't you think you're spending too much time with them? I thought we were doing something tonight."

Megan had tried to explain, tried to tell Eliza that it was just a dinner, a professional gathering. But Eliza's eyes darkened. "You're always so busy with them, Megan. Do you really need them more than me? You're mine, you know. I should be the one you want to spend your time with, not them."

The guilt was immediate, suffocating. Megan canceled the dinner, choosing to stay home with Eliza instead. That night, Eliza was more affectionate than ever, showering Megan with compliments, telling her she was the only one who truly understood her. Megan felt conflicted, torn between the relief of making Eliza happy and the nagging feeling that something wasn't quite right.

The more Megan tried to hold on to her connections with others, the more Eliza pushed back. Every time she mentioned a new project at work, a coffee date with an old friend, Eliza would pull away, using silence and distance as weapons. It was as if every moment spent outside their shared world felt like a betrayal. Eliza made sure to remind Megan of how lucky she was to have someone who loved her the way she did. "You know," Eliza would murmur, "I'd do anything for you. I just want you to remember that. No one else is ever going to care about you the way I do."

And slowly, Megan began to believe it. She didn't want to lose Eliza, and she didn't want to be accused of neglecting her. She found herself canceling plans, turning down invitations, and making excuses for missing time with her friends. Each time she did, Eliza would be there, waiting, ready to shower her with affection, convincing her that everything was just as it should be. But the pattern grew clearer. Megan was slowly, but surely, losing herself.

Then one day, Megan ran into Sarah at the coffee shop, an unexpected encounter that left her feeling momentarily free. They caught up on old times, reminiscing about their shared memories. But as Megan left, a strange sense of dread washed over her. She had enjoyed their time together, but the guilt gnawed at her, reminding her of the unspoken rules in her relationship with Eliza.

That evening, Eliza was quieter than usual, and Megan couldn't shake the feeling that something was wrong. When they sat down to eat, Eliza finally spoke, her voice calm but laced with an unsettling edge. "I saw you with Sarah today," Eliza said, her eyes fixed on Megan's. "You know, you're always with her. I don't think I can trust you when you're spending so much time with someone who isn't me."

Megan felt her stomach drop. "What are you talking about? Sarah's just a friend," she said, her voice trembling. "You know she's been in my life for years."

Eliza's lips curled into a cold smile. "I'm not the one who needs reassurance, Megan. You're the one who has to explain yourself. I just want to make sure you know who comes first. And you're starting to forget that. You're starting to forget me."

The words hit Megan harder than she had anticipated. She hadn't realized how far things had gone, how much Eliza had already controlled her world. The manipulations, the isolations—they were all just part of Eliza's game. Every accusation, every request for reassurance, every claim that Megan didn't love her enough—it was all a tool to push her deeper into dependence.

In that moment, Megan realized that she had already lost everything. Her career, her friendships, her sense of self—they were all gone, buried under the weight of Eliza's jealousy. And when she looked at Eliza, her heart sinking, she understood the darkest truth: Eliza wasn't just jealous. She had used jealousy as a weapon, a way to make Megan question her worth, to isolate her from everything that had once mattered, until there was nothing left but Eliza's control.

Megan had played into it. She had been complicit in her own undoing. And now, as she sat there across from Eliza, her heart heavy with the weight of it all, she knew there was no way back. There was no one left to save her but herself—and by then, she wasn't sure if she had the strength to escape.

The Invisible Standard

Maya had always considered herself an independent person. She had her own job, her own friends, and her own life. She didn't need anyone to complete her—at least, that's what she had always believed. But when she met Laura, something shifted. Laura was everything Maya wasn't—bold, charming, and effortlessly confident. She made Maya feel special in ways she had never known. Laura seemed to have a way of making everything seem possible, making Maya feel like the center of her universe.

At first, things were easy. They spent long nights talking about everything and nothing, sharing their fears and their dreams. Laura made Maya laugh, made her feel seen. It felt like the kind of relationship that Maya had always wanted, one where every day was a promise of something better. But as the months passed, things started to change. It was subtle at first—a look, a comment that seemed almost too small to notice, but the shift in the air was undeniable.

"Maya, why didn't you get the bigger size?" Laura asked one night, glancing at the dress Maya had chosen at the store. "It's such a shame, I think it would've looked better on you. You want to look good for me, don't you?"

Maya felt a sting of discomfort but brushed it off. "I thought this would be fine. It's not that important, right?"

But Laura's eyes narrowed, and the smile she gave her felt forced. "Of course, it's important. You should always want to look your best. For me."

That night, as Maya lay in bed, she couldn't help but wonder what Laura meant. She had never been someone overly concerned with her appearance, but if Laura thought it mattered, then maybe it did. Maybe she needed to pay more attention to how she presented herself. After all, Laura had never asked for anything unreasonable before.

As time went on, Maya found herself doing more and more to meet Laura's ever-growing list of unspoken expectations. It wasn't just about appearances anymore. It was about her behavior, too. "You really should spend more time on your career, Maya," Laura would say. "You know I believe in you, but you could be so much more. I want you to be someone who has everything, who doesn't settle for mediocrity. You're too smart to stay where you are."

Maya tried to focus on her work more, sacrificing nights with friends and time for herself to live up to what Laura seemed to want. But every time she thought she was meeting Laura's standards, there was something else. "Why don't you just call your mom?" Laura would ask, her voice laced with irritation. "Don't you think you should check in with her more? Or is she not important to you?"

Maya would feel the weight of guilt settle in. She hadn't talked to her mom in a while, but every time she thought about reaching out, there was this nagging feeling that she should be doing more, something that would show Laura that she was giving her the attention she deserved.

And so, Maya would spend the next few days trying to meet Laura's unspoken demands. She worked longer hours, spent more time making sure everything around the house was perfect, tried harder to call her mom, and focused on looking her best when Laura was around. It felt like a constant balancing act, but she did it because Laura had made her feel like it was what was expected. But each time Maya thought she had done enough, something new would surface.

"I just don't understand why you can't take things more seriously," Laura said one evening as they sat together on the couch. "I'm doing everything I can to help you. Don't you want to succeed? Don't you want to be more than you are right now?"

Maya blinked, stunned. She had been trying so hard. Wasn't that enough? Wasn't she enough?

"I'm doing my best, Laura. I really am. I just—" Maya's voice faltered, the frustration bubbling over. "But what is it that you really want from me?"

Laura's expression changed in an instant, the frustration turning to something colder, sharper. "You really don't get it, do you? You just don't try hard enough. You could have all of it, but you don't seem to care about the things that matter. If you loved me, you would understand. I shouldn't have to tell you these things."

Maya's heart dropped. She had done everything—everything she thought Laura wanted. But now, it seemed like nothing was ever enough. She felt lost, trapped in a cycle of trying to fulfill expectations that had never been clearly set.

Days turned into weeks, and the weight of it all began to wear on her. She stopped seeing her friends. She canceled plans with her family. She worked herself into exhaustion, hoping that each day she would meet Laura's standards. But nothing changed. Every gesture, every effort, was met with something new.

One night, after coming home late from work, Maya collapsed onto the couch, exhausted. Laura didn't even look up from her phone. She hadn't said much to Maya all evening, and now, there was a coldness in the air. "You didn't pick up dinner," Laura said after a long silence, her tone clipped.

Maya's stomach sank. "I thought we could just order something later, I didn't know you wanted it now—"

"You don't understand, do you?" Laura's voice was suddenly sharp. "You just keep disappointing me, Maya. You never think ahead. I've been doing all this work, all this for us, and you can't even do one thing right. I don't even know why I keep trying."

Maya felt the tears start to form, but she quickly wiped them away. She had tried. She had tried everything.

That night, she lay awake, staring at the ceiling, her mind racing. She had given up so much of herself, trying to live up to an ideal she couldn't reach. She didn't even know what Laura truly wanted from her anymore. And yet, despite everything, she stayed. Because somewhere deep inside, she was terrified of the idea that if she couldn't meet those demands, she would lose Laura. She would lose the person who had made her feel special in the beginning.

But as Maya drifted off to sleep, something inside her shifted. She realized that in trying so desperately to meet an invisible standard, she had lost who she was. The person she had been before Laura's expectations took root was slipping further away. And she didn't know how much more of herself she could give before there was nothing left.

And as the days passed, Maya understood the harsh truth: the more she tried, the less she became. The expectations were never meant to be fulfilled—they were designed to break her.

The Perfect Lie

When Nora met Lily, she felt like she had finally found someone who saw her for who she truly was. Lily was everything Nora had ever wanted—beautiful, confident, and effortlessly kind. At first, it was as if the universe had finally aligned for Nora. Lily's smile was bright, her words thoughtful, and her touch tender in a way that made Nora feel like she was the most important person in the world. Every time they talked, Lily made Nora feel seen, adored, and appreciated. She couldn't believe her luck.

Nora had always been cautious in love, hesitant to dive in too deeply, afraid of being hurt. But with Lily, everything felt different. There was a sense of ease in their connection, a natural flow that made Nora believe that this was it—this was the one. Lily told her everything that Nora had always longed to hear. "You're the most amazing woman I've ever met," Lily would say, gazing at her with such intensity that Nora believed every word. "I'm so lucky to have found someone like you. You're perfect for me."

And so, Nora let herself fall. Slowly at first, but completely. Lily seemed to love her in a way that felt like a dream come true. She would surprise Nora with flowers, cook her dinner, and show up with small thoughtful gifts. Every gesture, every word, made Nora feel special, as though she had finally found her place in the world. She felt cherished. She felt adored.

But over time, the small cracks began to form. Lily's behavior started to shift, but in ways that were so subtle, Nora could almost convince herself that it was normal. Lily would become upset over the smallest things. If Nora made plans without consulting her first, Lily would pout, telling her that it hurt her feelings. "I just want to be with you," Lily would say, her voice soft but laced with something darker. "Why does it feel like I'm not enough?"

Nora would apologize, every time, even when she hadn't done anything wrong. She didn't want to upset Lily, didn't want to make her feel abandoned. Lily would smile again, but there was something in her eyes that made Nora uneasy, a flicker of something possessive that she couldn't quite place. But she brushed it off, told herself she was being paranoid. After all, Lily had been nothing but perfect for her.

Then the emotional manipulation began. It was small at first—an offhand comment here and there, a criticism veiled as concern. "You know, you don't really spend enough time with me when you go out with your friends," Lily would say one evening, her tone calm but tinged with something sharper. "I don't want to feel like I'm competing for your attention."

Nora, feeling guilty, would immediately start canceling plans, rearranging her life to accommodate Lily's needs. But no matter what she did, it was never enough. The guilt grew heavier. "I just want to be enough for you," Lily would say, always with a sigh, as though she were the one being wronged. "But sometimes, I feel like you'd rather be with everyone else. It's hard for me when you're not here."

Nora began to doubt herself. She loved Lily so much, and Lily had made her feel like the center of her world from the beginning. She wanted to make her happy. But no matter how much she gave, Lily's needs seemed endless, her demands growing more and more unreasonable. Slowly, Nora's world began to shrink. She stopped seeing her friends, stopped going out without Lily, stopped doing things she once enjoyed—just to keep Lily happy.

And then, Lily started revealing darker parts of herself. One evening, when Nora had forgotten to text her back right away, Lily became distant. "I don't understand why you couldn't just reply," she said, her voice flat. "Do I mean so little to you that I'm not even worth a simple message? I just need to know that I matter to you, Nora."

The words stung. They were so gentle, so understated, but they carried a weight that made Nora's chest tighten. "Of course you matter," Nora said, trying to reassure her. "I just got caught up at work."

But Lily wasn't satisfied. She began to bring up her past relationships, always comparing herself to the women Nora had been with before. "I don't think they really loved you like I do," Lily would say, her voice tinged with bitterness. "They didn't give you the kind of attention you deserve. But I'm here now. I'll always give you everything you need."

Nora would feel a pang of discomfort, but at the same time, the overwhelming desire to keep Lily happy kept her in line. She began to wonder if maybe Lily was right. Maybe the women from her past hadn't treated her well enough, hadn't really cared the way Lily did. Maybe this was just how love was supposed to feel.

Then one night, after an argument about nothing in particular, Lily pushed Nora away, the coldness in her voice a stark contrast to the warmth that had once drawn Nora in. "I don't know if I can keep doing this," Lily said, her eyes darting away, avoiding Nora's gaze. "You're just not as attentive as I need you to be. I feel like you're pulling away from me."

Nora's stomach dropped. "I'm not pulling away. I just—" She tried to explain, but Lily cut her off.

"I need someone who will put me first," Lily said sharply, her voice taking on a cutting edge. "If you can't do that, I don't know how we can keep going. It hurts too much."

Nora felt like she was drowning. She had tried so hard to be perfect, to meet every unspoken expectation, and yet it was never enough. No matter what she did, it felt like she was falling short. She couldn't understand what she had done wrong. She had given everything to Lily, and now, the person she had come to love so deeply was withdrawing, pulling away, blaming her for not fulfilling needs she hadn't even known existed.

The next day, Lily was distant, colder than she had ever been before. It was as if a wall had been built between them, a wall that Nora couldn't climb. "I'm not sure I can do this anymore," Lily said, her voice emotionless. "Maybe we should just take a break. I don't think you're ready to give me what I need."

Nora's heart shattered. She had tried so hard, so desperately, to be the perfect partner for Lily. She had sacrificed everything for their relationship, yet nothing ever seemed to be enough. She realized, too late, that the perfection she had sought wasn't love—it was control. Lily had made her believe that the love she received came with conditions, that the only way to earn it was to be someone she wasn't. And now, as Lily stepped back further and further, Nora could see the truth: there had never been love—just manipulation, just a perfect lie.

And as the darkness settled in, Nora understood that she had given up too much of herself to be with someone who had never truly loved her. She had fallen for the illusion, and now, the emptiness was all that was left.

The Isolation Project

Rachel had always been an independent person, someone who thrived on her friendships and family connections. She had always believed that love should be a partnership, a shared experience where both people could grow, support each other, and find strength in their own individual worlds. That was until she met Julia.

Julia was magnetic, an enigma wrapped in kindness and charm. She made Rachel feel seen in ways she had never felt before, like she was the only person in the world who mattered. From the first time they met, Julia was a presence that made everything feel lighter. Her compliments were like small acts of salvation, her touch a gentle reassurance. Rachel had never known someone so attuned to her needs. It didn't take long before Julia became the center of Rachel's world.

In the beginning, everything felt perfect. Julia would surprise Rachel with thoughtful gestures—flowers, handwritten notes, unexpected getaways. She would tell Rachel how lucky she was to have found someone like her, someone so beautiful, so intelligent, so worthy of love. It felt like they were building something extraordinary, something that could never be torn apart. Rachel was content to give Julia all her attention, believing that this was love, pure and simple.

But slowly, Julia began to make small requests. At first, they seemed harmless. "Do you really need to talk to Sarah again tonight? She's always been so critical of you," Julia would say, her voice light but tinged with concern. "I think it's better when it's just the two of us, don't you?"

Rachel would brush it off at first, dismissing it as a small quirk in Julia's personality, an innocent insecurity. But as time went on, Julia's comments became more frequent, more pointed. When Rachel went to visit her parents, Julia would be quiet for days afterward. "You know, your mom never really understood you," she would say. "I can't help but feel like they don't respect the life you've built with me. I just want to make sure you're putting the right people first."

Rachel was unsettled, but she tried to ignore the nagging feeling in her chest. She'd always been close to her family and friends, and she wanted to believe that Julia's words were just part of her desire to feel secure in their relationship. But slowly, she began to feel that Julia's love came with conditions—conditions that required her to distance herself from those she loved most.

The weeks passed, and Rachel started finding herself making excuses for not seeing her friends, for not talking to her family. Julia's comments grew harsher and more insistent. "Sarah really isn't good for you, Rachel," Julia would say, her voice tight with something unspoken. "She's always been so negative. You know, she's just holding you back. You don't need her. You need me."

At first, Rachel pushed back. "She's my best friend, Julia. We've known each other for years. I can't just stop seeing her."

Julia would stare at her for a long moment, her gaze cold and intense, before finally softening. "I just don't want to see you hurt, Rachel. She's been through so much, but she's not the one who's going to be there for you the way I am."

Rachel, feeling guilty and torn, began to pull away from Sarah, from her parents, from her friends. Each time, Julia would be there, with comforting words, with soothing gestures, telling Rachel that she was doing the right thing. "You're the most important person in my life," Julia would say, "and I'm just trying to protect you. You deserve so much better than the people who don't see you the way I do."

And so, Rachel started to believe it. She started to believe that Julia was the only one who truly cared for her, that the world outside of their relationship was a threat to the love they shared. She stopped answering calls from Sarah, canceled dinner plans with her parents, and made excuses for not attending gatherings with friends. Slowly, her world began to shrink, and the people who had once been her support system faded into the background.

Julia's influence grew stronger. Rachel found herself canceling more and more of her own plans, constantly making sure that Julia's needs were met before her own. She couldn't remember the last time she'd felt like herself, like she was in control of her life. Every decision seemed to run through Julia first, and if Rachel didn't act in a way that met Julia's approval, the guilt would eat away at her.

One night, after Rachel had missed yet another call from Sarah, she sat down to try to explain herself to Julia. "I've been so focused on you," Rachel began, her voice trembling. "I don't want to lose my friends, Julia. I don't want to push everyone away, but I don't know how to fix it."

Julia sat down beside her, her eyes soft, her touch gentle. "I don't want you to feel guilty, Rachel. I'm not trying to control you. I just want you to see what's important. The people who really care about you—they don't have your best interests at heart the way I do. They won't understand our love, and you deserve someone who will always put you first. Don't you want that?"

Rachel's heart twisted. She didn't want to believe it, but deep down, she knew that Julia was right. She was the one who had been there for her. She was the one who understood her. And without Julia, who else would care? Who else would love her in this way?

As the days went on, Rachel found herself slipping further into isolation. She stopped questioning Julia's motives, stopped feeling the need to explain herself. She couldn't remember the last time she had a real conversation with Sarah, or the last time she laughed with her parents. Julia had become her world. And in the quiet moments, when Julia wasn't around, Rachel felt a gnawing emptiness, as if a part of her was missing, but the thought of leaving Julia was too frightening. How could she possibly walk away from the one person who seemed to understand her?

One afternoon, after Rachel had finished yet another call with her mother where she made excuses for not visiting, she looked in the mirror. The person staring back at her was someone she barely recognized. She had become someone else, someone entirely defined by Julia's needs and expectations.

And as the realization settled in, Rachel knew, in the deepest part of her being, that she would never be able to break free. Not now. Not after everything Julia had done. She had been systematically isolated, cut off from the people who had once supported her, and now, she was alone—completely dependent on Julia for validation, for love.

Julia had done exactly what she intended. She had slowly, methodically, made Rachel believe that there was no one left to trust, no one left to care for her, except for her. And now, with nothing but Julia's voice in her ears, Rachel understood the cruel truth: She wasn't in a relationship. She was in a prison.

The Cost of Care

When Olivia first met Jane, she was everything Jane had ever wanted. Confident, poised, and always able to take charge in any situation, Olivia had a way of making Jane feel safe in a way she hadn't felt in years. At first, Jane was drawn to Olivia's strength and independence—qualities she admired and wanted to emulate. But it wasn't long before Olivia's subtle vulnerabilities began to emerge, and Jane, ever the caretaker, found herself eager to fill the role of the loving, supportive partner.

Olivia would often make little comments about how tired she felt, how overwhelmed by work, or how difficult things were at home. Jane, in turn, would offer her support, listening intently, comforting Olivia with her reassuring words. It felt good to be needed, to be the one who could take away Olivia's burdens. "You're always here for me," Olivia would say, her voice soft, full of affection. "I don't know what I would do without you."

At first, it felt like love. Jane wanted to make Olivia happy, wanted to be the person who could ease Olivia's struggles. She was the one Olivia turned to, the one who always knew how to make things better. But as time went on, Olivia's needs began to take on a different shape.

It started small. Olivia began to complain about the smallest of things: a headache, a sore throat, a slight fever. At first, Jane thought little of it. Everyone got sick sometimes. But when Olivia's symptoms started to become more frequent and intense, Jane couldn't ignore it. Olivia would lie in bed for days, weak and fragile, complaining of fatigue that never seemed to go away. Jane would cancel her own plans, take time off work, and devote herself entirely to caring for Olivia. She believed it was out of love. After all, Olivia was the most important thing in her life.

But as the days stretched into weeks, Jane started to feel the weight of it all. She couldn't remember the last time she'd done something for herself, the last time she'd seen her friends, or spent time on her hobbies. Olivia's illness had consumed them both. Olivia would complain about feeling worse, about being too tired to get out of bed, and Jane would be there, always by her side, constantly reassuring her that she was doing everything right.

"I can't keep up anymore," Jane said one evening, her voice tinged with exhaustion. "I've been taking care of you nonstop, and I don't know how much more I can do. I haven't seen anyone in weeks."

Olivia, still lying in bed with a cold compress on her forehead, opened her eyes, looking at Jane with a soft, vulnerable expression. "I know you're tired," she said, her voice trembling slightly. "I'm so sorry to be a burden, Jane. But I don't know how to get better without you. You're the only one who can help me. I'm nothing without you."

The words were laced with guilt, and Jane couldn't help but feel it—the overwhelming sense of duty to Olivia. She wanted to be the strong partner, the one who was always there, who could fix things. Olivia's illness had become the glue that held them together, and the more Jane tried to pull away, the more Olivia seemed to need her. Jane could not bear the thought of leaving Olivia alone, could not imagine walking away when Olivia was so fragile, so dependent.

But things began to unravel. Jane started to notice patterns, things that didn't add up. Olivia's illness seemed to come and go with alarming regularity. On some days, Olivia would be bedridden, barely able to move. On others, she would be up and about, doing small tasks around the house with no apparent signs of illness. Jane was confused, but every time she questioned it, Olivia would turn her eyes on her, full of guilt and sadness.

"You don't believe me?" Olivia would ask, her voice small and hurt. "You think I'm faking this, don't you?"

Jane would quickly apologize, feeling the sting of doubt she had allowed to surface. "No, I'm just worried. I don't know how to help you if you keep getting better and worse. I just want to see you feel better for good."

Olivia would smile weakly, but it was a smile that always seemed to hide something darker. "I'm just so tired, Jane. I'm really trying. But I need you to be here for me. I need you."

As the months went on, Jane's own health began to decline. She was exhausted, her once-vibrant life now reduced to a series of hospital visits, late nights caring for Olivia, and endless days spent trying to comfort someone who seemed to never improve. But Jane could never bring herself to leave, to step back and take a break. She had become so wrapped up in Olivia's needs, so consumed by the role of caretaker, that she had forgotten what it felt like to have a life outside of this.

One day, Jane walked into their bedroom to find Olivia sitting up in bed, scrolling through her phone, a bright smile on her face. "You're looking better," Jane said, her voice weak from exhaustion. "Are you feeling okay?"

Olivia looked up at her, her eyes twinkling with something Jane couldn't quite place. "I'm feeling fine," Olivia said, putting the phone down on the bedside table. "Just taking a break. I was thinking about going to lunch with some friends this weekend. Maybe you could join us."

The words hit Jane like a cold slap. Friends? Lunch? It had been months since Olivia had shown any interest in seeing anyone outside of their home, let alone making plans with friends. Jane's chest tightened. "You're going out with friends?" she asked, her voice trembling. "You said you were too sick for that. You've been in bed for days."

Olivia's expression shifted slightly, and Jane could see the flicker of something cold in her eyes. "You don't have to be here all the time, Jane," she said, her voice turning sharp. "I'm fine. I've been fine. I don't need you to babysit me. I've just been waiting for you to understand that I need a little space, too."

The realization crashed down on Jane. Olivia had been faking it all along. The illness, the fatigue, the endless need for attention—it had all been a game. A game to keep Jane dependent, to make her feel guilty for wanting something more than this. Olivia had controlled her every move, manipulated her into neglecting everything and everyone in her life, all in the name of love and care.

"Why didn't you tell me?" Jane whispered, her heart shattering. "Why did you make me believe that you needed me?"

Olivia looked at her with a smile, one that wasn't filled with love, but with something colder—something calculated. "Because it worked," she said softly. "You were the perfect pawn. And now, I have you exactly where I want you."

And in that moment, Jane understood. She had been the one who had built the cage, who had allowed herself to become trapped by Olivia's lies. The guilt, the sacrifice, the endless care—none of it had ever been about love. It had all been part of a plan, a manipulation so subtle that she hadn't seen it until it was too late.

Olivia was fine. But Jane had given up everything.

The Weight of Love

Rachel had always been the kind of person who put others first. She believed in selflessness, in sacrifice, in love that meant doing whatever it took to make someone else happy. She never minded taking a backseat to someone else's dreams, as long as they were happy. So when she met Lily, someone who needed her support in ways no one had ever needed before, she felt like she had found someone worth fighting for.

Lily was ambitious, driven, and consumed by her goals. She had dreams of building a successful career, of becoming someone who could change the world. Rachel admired that about her. She admired Lily's passion, her determination to push through every obstacle. But soon, Rachel noticed that Lily's ambitions came with a price—a price that Rachel was more than willing to pay.

It started small. Lily would ask Rachel to help her with late-night work sessions, to drive her to meetings, to listen to her talk about her struggles and frustrations. Rachel didn't mind. She loved being there for Lily, loved watching her chase her dreams. But slowly, the requests began to change. "I need you here more," Lily would say, her tone soft but insistent. "You're always so busy with your own things, Rachel. Don't you think you should be focusing on me? I can't do this without you."

Rachel's friends would ask why she hadn't been around lately. Her family started to notice the missed calls and canceled visits. But Rachel just shrugged it off. She was doing it all for Lily. Lily needed her. She was important. What else mattered?

As Lily's career began to take off, Rachel found herself giving up more and more of her own life. She quit her job, put her own dreams on hold, all so she could support Lily in every way possible. "You're my rock," Lily would say, her eyes full of gratitude. "I could never do this without you."

But the gratitude was short-lived. As Lily's career grew, so did her demands. Rachel would spend her days running errands, making sure Lily had everything she needed to succeed, while her own ambitions slowly faded into the background. There was always something else—another project to help with, another meeting to attend, another decision to be made. "You're so good at organizing things, Rachel. You're the only one who can do this for me," Lily would say. And Rachel, eager to please, would oblige, pushing her own goals further and further away.

The guilt crept in slowly. Rachel had always been a dreamer, someone who had wanted to write, to travel, to experience life outside of the shadow of someone else's success. But every time she even thought about picking up a pen or booking a flight, Lily would need her. Lily would be too busy, too stressed, too overwhelmed. "You don't mind, do you?" Lily would ask, her voice laced with something that made it impossible for Rachel to say no.

But then, as Lily's success snowballed, so did her indifference. Rachel would spend entire days alone, waiting for Lily to finish meetings, waiting for her to return phone calls, waiting for her to acknowledge how much she had sacrificed. But there was nothing. Lily was always too tired, too focused on her own world to notice Rachel's. It wasn't until Rachel had been sitting in silence for hours, waiting for Lily to take a break, that she realized how much of herself she had lost.

One evening, Rachel decided to confront her. She had kept quiet for so long, hidden behind the veil of selflessness, that she had no idea how to express what she felt. But as Lily talked about yet another upcoming trip, another event Rachel would have to plan, something inside her broke.

"I've been putting everything on hold for you, Lily," Rachel said, her voice trembling. "I've given up everything for you. My job, my life, my dreams. You don't even see it, do you?"

Lily looked up from her phone, an eyebrow raised, a slight smile playing on her lips. "What do you mean, Rachel? I appreciate everything you've done for me. I couldn't have gotten this far without you. But you knew this was the deal when we started, right? You knew what I needed."

Rachel stared at her, the weight of it sinking in. "I thought I was helping you. But I'm not. I've just been in the background of your life, pretending my own didn't matter."

Lily's face softened, but only for a moment. "You're being dramatic. I love you, Rachel. You're amazing. But I need you. How could you possibly think that giving up everything for me was a bad thing? I'm doing this for us. For our future."

Rachel's heart broke. She had always believed that the sacrifices she made were part of love. She had thought that helping Lily reach her dreams meant sharing in her success. But as Lily went on, describing the next step in her career, the next big move, Rachel realized that she had been nothing more than a stepping stone, an invisible support for someone else's dream.

And when she finally tried to voice her own needs, Lily just dismissed her as if she were being unreasonable. "You know I can't focus on you right now, Rachel," Lily said, her voice cold now, distant. "I'm building something here. I can't keep catering to your little fantasies. You knew what I was doing when you chose to stay."

Rachel looked at her, the years of her own ambitions slipping away. She realized, then, that Lily had never been interested in her goals, her desires. She had used Rachel's selflessness, her willingness to sacrifice, to keep herself at the center of everything. It wasn't love—it was manipulation.

As Rachel walked out of the room that night, the weight of what she had lost crushed her. She had given everything to someone who only cared about what she could provide, someone who never asked about her needs because they didn't matter. Rachel had been so focused on making Lily happy, on being the perfect partner, that she had lost herself completely.

In the end, Lily's success would continue. She would move forward, her career blossoming, while Rachel stood on the sidelines, watching the life she had once dreamed of slip further and further away. And Rachel realized, as she sat alone, that the sacrifices she had made were not acts of love—they were the cost of her own destruction.

The Strings You Pull

Mia had always prided herself on being a good judge of character. She was the kind of person who gave her trust cautiously but deeply once it was earned. When she met Ava, she was drawn to her calm demeanor, her understanding eyes, and the way she seemed to listen so carefully when Mia spoke. Ava was easy to talk to, and Mia felt comfortable with her in a way she hadn't with anyone else. It didn't take long for them to become inseparable—at least, that's what Mia thought.

Ava was supportive in all the right ways, or so it seemed. Whenever Mia expressed an interest in a new project, Ava would encourage her with quiet enthusiasm. "You're so talented, Mia," Ava would say. "You should do it. You deserve the success." Her words felt like a balm, soothing the insecurities Mia had carried for years. Ava was always there when Mia needed her, whether it was to listen after a tough day at work or to provide emotional support when Mia was unsure of herself.

But over time, something began to shift. Mia noticed the way Ava seemed to always steer conversations toward what *Ava* wanted. "You should really think about moving into a bigger place," Ava said one night, casually placing the idea into Mia's mind. "You deserve it, and with your promotion at work, it would be easy to afford. A bigger space would make us both feel more comfortable, don't you think?"

Mia hesitated. She had always been content in her cozy apartment. But Ava's words planted a seed of doubt. "I guess I've been thinking about it," Mia said, trying to dismiss the sudden anxiety growing inside her.

"You should," Ava replied with a smile, her eyes gleaming with something that Mia couldn't quite place. "You've been working so hard. You need more space to grow. You deserve more."

At first, Mia dismissed it as just one suggestion, one of many that Ava had made during their time together. But as the weeks went by, the suggestions became more frequent, more insistent. It wasn't just about moving to a bigger apartment anymore. "You know, Mia," Ava would say, "you've been working a lot lately, but I think you should think about scaling back. Maybe you could take a break from that job you hate so much. You could focus more on the things that matter. You're always so stressed, and I want you to be happy."

Mia's heart sank. She had worked hard to get her job, to make something of herself, and now Ava, who had always appeared so supportive, was questioning it. But when Mia pushed back, when she expressed concerns about her career and the steps she had taken, Ava would reassure her, "I just want you to be happy. I want us to be happy together."

It was the repeated promises of happiness, the whispered reassurances that Mia deserved to be free of the stress, that kept Mia questioning herself. Ava was so convincing, so gentle, that Mia began to wonder if maybe Ava was right. Maybe Mia *did* need to scale back, maybe she needed a change of pace. Maybe everything Ava said was true.

One evening, after Mia had agreed to look into moving into a new place, Ava brought up another subject. "You know, Mia," she began, her voice warm and inviting, "I've been thinking. With you moving, and with all the stress you're under, maybe you should take a step back and think about your priorities. I could help you more—help us both more—if you weren't so tied up in that job. And, honestly, you could be so much happier if you took some time to focus on yourself. I'd feel so much more secure if you could be with me more."

The words, though seemingly innocent, felt suffocating to Mia. She hadn't realized how much time she'd been giving up for Ava, how much of herself had already been swallowed by Ava's demands. But still, she hesitated. "I don't know, Ava," Mia said, her voice wavering. "I've worked hard to get where I am, and I can't just give up everything for you. I've made sacrifices for myself, too."

Ava's smile faltered for a second, but she quickly recovered, taking Mia's hand in hers. "I would never ask you to give up everything for me, Mia. But think about it—if we lived together in a bigger space, and you focused on what makes you happy, we could both thrive. We could build a future together, a future where you're not stressed and overworked. I just want you to feel supported."

That night, Mia couldn't sleep. The idea of sacrificing her career, her independence, for the sake of a future with Ava didn't sit right with her, but Ava's words echoed in her mind. Maybe she was being too stubborn. Maybe it was time to trust Ava, to believe that what Ava wanted for them was the right path. Slowly, the doubts that had once plagued Mia started to dissipate, and she began to believe that maybe Ava was right all along.

A month later, Mia had quit her job, signed a lease for a new, bigger apartment, and begun focusing solely on their relationship. Ava had been thrilled by the change. "I knew you'd come around," she said, holding Mia close, her voice filled with pride. "This is exactly what we need. Now we can build a life together. I'm so proud of you."

But as Mia settled into this new life, something started to feel wrong. She had nothing to distract her anymore, nothing to fill the hours like her career used to. She spent all her time with Ava, caring for the apartment, attending to Ava's needs, but the more Mia gave, the more she felt like she was losing herself.

It wasn't until she overheard a conversation between Ava and a friend that the truth finally hit. "She's so easy to manipulate," Ava said, laughing lightly. "I've got her exactly where I want her. I knew she'd give up everything for me if I played it right. She's so predictable."

The words crashed into Mia's mind, leaving her paralyzed. Ava had never wanted to build a life with her; she had used Mia's trust and love to isolate her, to make her dependent. All the sacrifices Mia had made, all the steps she had taken to please Ava, had been for nothing. She had been manipulated, not cared for, not loved.

As the realization sank in, Mia felt like she had no choice but to stay. Her life had been restructured entirely around Ava's agenda. She had no job, no friends, and no family left. Ava had orchestrated it all, piece by piece. And Mia, trapped in the perfect lie, now had nowhere to turn.

The walls that had been built around her were closing in, and for the first time, Mia understood the true cost of her sacrifice. She was no longer herself; she was just a pawn in Ava's game. And there was no way out.

The Fall and Rise

Clara had always been the steady one, the dependable one. She liked to think of herself as someone who had everything figured out—at least, that's what she tried to portray. When she met Amanda, something shifted. Amanda was unlike anyone Clara had ever known—flawed yet captivating, unpredictable yet magnetic. It wasn't long before Clara was pulled into Amanda's world, a world that was filled with moments of intensity, passion, and laughter. At first, it was like a whirlwind, and Clara couldn't help but be swept away.

Amanda's charm was like a drug. One moment, she would be soft and loving, showering Clara with affection, telling her how much she meant to her, how perfect they were together. "I've never felt like this before," Amanda would say, her eyes sparkling with something that felt real. "You're everything I've been looking for. I can't imagine my life without you."

Clara, starved for someone to truly see her, would bask in the warmth of Amanda's words. But then, just when Clara felt like she had found her place, Amanda would pull away. "I don't know, Clara," she'd say, her voice suddenly distant. "I just don't feel the same anymore. I need space. I think we're moving too fast."

The shift would come without warning, and Clara would be left reeling. She would spend days wondering what went wrong, trying to figure out how to fix it, trying to win back the affection she had once felt so certain of. And then, just when she thought she was losing Amanda for good, Amanda would come back—sweet, tender, apologetic. "I've been thinking about us," Amanda would say, tracing a finger down Clara's arm. "I'm sorry for pulling away. I just... I need you. You mean everything to me."

And Clara, eager to be wanted, would fall for it every time. The cycle began—this constant back-and-forth, the highs and lows, the emotional peaks and valleys. Amanda would make Clara feel on top of the world one moment, and the next, she'd have her questioning everything. Clara would chase the moments when Amanda was affectionate, when she made Clara feel important. She lived for those moments, the fleeting moments of warmth and connection, desperately trying to hold onto them, even as they always slipped through her fingers.

As the weeks passed, the cycle intensified. Clara found herself walking on eggshells, constantly second-guessing herself, afraid of saying or doing the wrong thing. She'd learned to read Amanda's moods, to feel the subtle shift in the air before Amanda would withdraw. Clara's heart would race, and she would do whatever it took to keep Amanda close. She would apologize for things she didn't even understand, trying to fix what wasn't broken, trying to make things right. The emotional treadmill had taken hold of her, and no matter how hard she ran, she couldn't escape it.

Amanda would become increasingly distant, always pulling away just when Clara thought things were going well. "I don't know if this is really what I want," Amanda would murmur, her tone vague but pointed. "Maybe we're just not meant to be."

Clara would plead, her voice breaking. "But we were fine last week! You said you loved me. You said I was everything."

Amanda would look away, her gaze cold, and Clara would feel like she was losing everything. The sudden withdrawal would leave Clara feeling empty, hollow, as though she had been left in the dark. And just when the darkness seemed unbearable, Amanda would return—sweet, apologetic, full of promises.

"I'm sorry," Amanda would say, her voice full of tenderness. "I didn't mean to hurt you. I just get scared sometimes. I need you more than you know. I love you."

And Clara would believe it, would believe in the love that Amanda was offering, would believe that they were meant to be. In that moment, Clara would feel like the luckiest person alive. The warmth would return, the intensity, the passion. But she never knew how long it would last. The cycle always started again, and she found herself in the same emotional trap—constantly chasing after something that was never stable, never certain.

It wasn't until Clara found herself standing in front of a mirror, her reflection staring back at her with vacant eyes, that she realized how far she had fallen. She had become someone else, someone who no longer knew who she was without Amanda. She had lost herself in the roller coaster of highs and lows, of love and abandonment. The love she had so desperately wanted had turned into a prison. She had become addicted to the fleeting moments when Amanda made her feel like she mattered, when Amanda told her she was loved.

Clara sat on the edge of their bed, waiting for Amanda to return. Her heart pounded as she listened to the silence, the ache of longing and confusion heavy in her chest. She had given everything—her time, her energy, her sense of self—and yet, she was still waiting for Amanda to choose her, to stay, to love her completely. But she knew deep down that it would never happen. The cycle would continue, the emotional treadmill would keep spinning, and she would keep running, forever chasing the moments that Amanda promised.

When Amanda walked through the door, her eyes light but distant, Clara barely looked up. "I've been thinking," Amanda said, her voice almost too casual, too detached. "Maybe we should take a break. I don't know if I'm ready for this."

The words hit Clara like a slap, but she said nothing. She had been waiting for this moment, the moment when the emotional high would crash. But this time, it felt different. The weight of it all finally hit her, and she realized she had been chasing something that wasn't real. Amanda's love had never been real. It had been a mirage, something that only existed to keep Clara running, never allowing her to stop and breathe, never allowing her to have peace.

Amanda's absence felt deafening as Clara sat in the silence of their room, the darkness swallowing her whole. For the first time, Clara understood the painful truth—she had given up everything for a love that never existed, for a person who would never stay. And as the quiet continued to stretch on, Clara understood the bitter lesson: she had been running on an emotional treadmill all along, and now, there was no way off.

Fractured Mirror

Maya had always been a quiet person, reserved but content in the life she had built for herself. Her friends admired her for her loyalty, her work ethic, and her ability to listen without judgment. But it wasn't until she met Zoe that Maya started questioning her own worth. Zoe was everything Maya was not—outgoing, confident, effortlessly charming. Zoe's laugh was infectious, and her smile could light up a room. At first, Maya found herself captivated by Zoe's presence, charmed by her enthusiasm and the way she seemed to see the world with such clarity.

It didn't take long for Zoe to sweep Maya off her feet. Zoe was affectionate, always showering Maya with compliments, always making her feel special. "You're different, Maya," Zoe would say, gazing at her with a warmth that made Maya feel like she was the center of the universe. "You're so much more than you realize. You just need someone to see it."

Maya's heart swelled at the thought of being seen, truly seen, by someone like Zoe. She had never been the center of attention before, and it felt good to be admired. But as the days went by, Maya began to notice subtle shifts in Zoe's behavior—shifts that seemed harmless at first, but as time went on, they chipped away at Maya's confidence, little by little.

Zoe would make small comments about Maya's appearance, always framed as concern or advice. "I think you'd look so much better if you wore a little more makeup," Zoe would say casually as they got ready for a night out. "I just don't get why you don't want to highlight your eyes. They're your best feature."

Maya would smile awkwardly, always feeling a pang of discomfort at Zoe's comments, but she brushed it off. Zoe was just trying to help, right? Maya had never been someone who paid attention to makeup or fashion. It was never her thing. But the more Zoe spoke about it, the more Maya found herself questioning her own choices, her own appearance. Maybe Zoe was right. Maybe she could look better, be better, if she just listened.

As time passed, Zoe's remarks became sharper, more frequent. "Don't you think you're being a bit too sensitive?" Zoe would say when Maya would express discomfort about something. "I mean, why are you always so defensive? You're just making things harder than they need to be."

Maya began to doubt her reactions, second-guessing her every word. Was she being too sensitive? Was she overreacting to things that shouldn't bother her? She started to feel like she was walking a tightrope around Zoe, constantly adjusting herself to meet her expectations, unsure of where she stood, unsure of who she was anymore.

Then, one night, as they sat together on the couch, Zoe made a comment that stuck with Maya like a shard of glass. "You know, my ex always knew how to handle things better than you do," Zoe said, not even looking up from her phone. "She didn't overthink everything. She just did what needed to be done."

Maya's stomach churned. "I don't—"

"No, no, don't get defensive," Zoe interrupted, her voice soft but laced with something colder. "I'm just saying, she was more confident in the way she handled things. I think you overcomplicate everything. You could be so much more if you didn't second-guess yourself all the time."

Maya swallowed hard, the words piercing deeper than she cared to admit. She had always struggled with self-doubt, with insecurity, but hearing Zoe compare her to an ex in such a casual way felt like a gut punch. She couldn't stop thinking about it, replaying the words over and over in her mind. Was she really so unsure of herself? Was she so inadequate?

From that moment on, Zoe's critiques became more personal. She would criticize the way Maya dressed, the way she spoke, even the way she laughed. "It's cute, but you should really be more elegant when you laugh," Zoe would say. "You're so much better than that."

Maya began to withdraw into herself, shrinking away from Zoe's judgment. She stopped speaking up when something bothered her, afraid of the backlash. When Zoe asked her to do something, Maya did it without question, without hesitation, hoping to avoid criticism. She would look in the mirror every morning, wondering if she looked good enough, if she was doing enough, if she was good enough.

And then one day, Zoe made a comment that shattered the final piece of Maya's confidence. "I just don't get why you don't have more friends," Zoe said, her voice almost gentle. "You're a great person, but I think people don't take you seriously. You don't really stand up for yourself, you know? Maybe that's why you don't connect with anyone on a deeper level."

Maya felt the weight of those words. She had always been more reserved, more comfortable in small groups or one-on-one conversations, but now, Zoe had made her feel like her introversion was a flaw. Like she was lacking something essential, something that others had and she didn't. The self-doubt spiraled, and for the first time, Maya couldn't ignore the cold truth: she was no longer the person she had once been.

She stopped reaching out to her friends, stopped taking risks, stopped doing anything that might invite criticism. She was so terrified of Zoe's judgment, so terrified of not measuring up, that she lost herself entirely.

The emotional weight of the constant critique wore her down, and she became a shell of the woman she had once been. She didn't recognize herself anymore, didn't know what she wanted or who she was. She was too scared to leave, too scared to speak up, too scared to even stand up for herself. All she could do was try harder to fit into the mold Zoe had created for her.

One day, after months of barely speaking to her friends, Maya received a text from one of them, asking her how she was doing. Maya stared at the screen, unsure of how to respond. She wanted to reach out, to talk, but a heavy weight in her chest kept her silent. What would she even say?

As she stared at the phone, the realization hit her with the force of a wrecking ball. Zoe hadn't just critiqued her appearance or her actions. She had broken her. She had torn down Maya's self-esteem piece by piece, making her feel like she wasn't enough. The constant comparisons, the undermining comments, the subtle manipulations—they had all been a way to control her, to make Maya believe she was nothing without Zoe.

And in that moment, Maya understood what Zoe had done: she had made her believe that she wasn't worthy of anyone's love but Zoe's, that she couldn't stand on her own.

The phone buzzed again, but this time, Maya didn't reach for it. Instead, she looked in the mirror, searching for the person she used to be. And as the silence settled around her, she realized the only thing left to do was to stop waiting for Zoe's approval and start finding her way back to herself.

The Silent Betrayal

Anna had always been the kind of person who trusted easily. She had a quiet confidence, and her relationships—whether with friends or family—were built on honesty and openness. She had never doubted the loyalty of those around her, had never questioned anyone's motives. That was, until she met Eliza.

Eliza was captivating. Charismatic and persuasive, she quickly became Anna's world. In the beginning, their relationship was everything Anna had dreamed of. Eliza was warm, affectionate, and made Anna feel valued in ways she had never felt before. She would listen to Anna's every word, validate her feelings, and tell her how lucky she was to have found someone so genuine. "I've never met anyone like you, Anna," Eliza would say. "You make me feel like I can trust again."

For the first few months, Anna was in awe of Eliza. She loved how Eliza always seemed to know exactly what to say, how she made Anna feel seen and understood. It was intoxicating, the way Eliza's compliments felt like a balm to Anna's soul. It was the kind of love Anna had always wanted, and she thought she had found it in Eliza.

But then, slowly, things began to shift. At first, it was subtle. One night, after a quiet dinner with Anna's best friend, Sarah, Eliza's voice was laced with concern. "You know, Sarah seems a little too interested in you," she said, her eyes narrowing slightly. "I mean, she's always touching you, always asking questions about us. Don't you think that's a little strange?"

Anna had always been close with Sarah, and she dismissed Eliza's words. "Sarah's my best friend. She's always like that. She just cares about me."

But Eliza's tone was insistent. "I just think it's a little much. She might be crossing boundaries. You should watch out. People can get too close and then hurt you."

Anna didn't know what to think. She trusted Sarah, but Eliza's concerns lingered in the back of her mind, and slowly, a seed of doubt began to take root.

As time passed, Eliza's suggestions grew more pointed. Anna's family, her colleagues, even the mailman—they all became potential threats. "You know," Eliza would say, casually, "I saw how Mark looked at you at that work event. I don't know what it was, but something felt off. You should be careful around him. I don't think he's as innocent as he seems."

Anna would try to shrug it off, but the subtle insinuations had an effect. Every interaction with someone—whether it was a friendly chat with a neighbor or a coffee break with a co-worker—began to feel charged. Anna found herself second-guessing every look, every word, wondering if there was something she was missing. Eliza's voice was always in the back of her mind, telling her that everyone around her had an ulterior motive.

The once confident, trusting Anna began to crumble under the weight of her own doubts. She started questioning Sarah's motives, wondering if the closeness they shared had been one-sided, wondering if Mark's friendly gestures had meant something more. Eliza's gentle nudging had worked—she had made Anna doubt herself and the people she loved.

But it didn't stop there. As Anna's world grew smaller, Eliza became more insistent on being the sole person Anna could rely on. "You don't need anyone else," Eliza would whisper, holding Anna close. "You have me. I've been through this before, Anna. People are selfish. They hurt you. But I'll never do that. I'm always going to be here for you."

Anna had always prided herself on being independent, on having a solid network of friends and family. But with every word, Eliza pushed her away from that support, convincing her that the only person who truly understood her, the only one she could trust, was Eliza. The isolation was gradual but relentless. Anna stopped seeing Sarah as often, stopped reaching out to her family, started avoiding work events. She began to focus only on Eliza, convinced that no one else could be trusted.

One day, Anna received a message from Sarah, asking to meet up for lunch. It had been weeks since they had seen each other, and something inside Anna stirred—a desire to reconnect, to talk about everything that had been building inside her. But as she read the message, Eliza's voice echoed in her mind. *Sarah's always been too clingy. She's too possessive of you. She can't be trusted.*

Anna hesitated. She thought about the last time they spoke, when Sarah had asked why she had been distant, why she hadn't responded to messages. Anna had made excuses, brushed it off as work stress, but now she couldn't shake the doubt that Eliza had planted in her.

She put the phone down without replying to Sarah.

Days later, Eliza made a comment that sealed Anna's doubt. "I saw Sarah walking down the street today," Eliza said, her voice casual but sharp. "She looked like she was on her way to your place. I just thought you should know. She's probably worried, right? She doesn't like that you've been spending so much time with me."

The comment hit Anna hard, even though it was delivered with a calm smile. She hadn't realized it before, but now it was clear: Sarah was the one trying to come between them. Sarah was the one causing the distance. She had to be. Eliza had never lied to her. Eliza had only tried to protect her.

From that point on, Anna's interactions with Sarah were strained. The calls became less frequent, the messages shorter. Whenever Sarah reached out, Anna would find an excuse to avoid her, to justify why they couldn't meet up. Sarah's attempts to reconnect only served to confirm Eliza's warnings: *She's trying to take you away from me. She doesn't really care about you the way I do.*

The trust Anna had once had in Sarah, in her family, in her co-workers, had withered away. All that was left was Eliza, her constant presence, her constant voice, telling Anna that everyone around her was deceitful, that the only person who truly loved her was Eliza. And Anna, lost and confused, had come to believe it.

Months later, as Anna sat alone, staring at the empty apartment that had once been a place of comfort, the realization hit her: she had been manipulated. Eliza had quietly, steadily, woven a web of lies that had isolated her from everyone who cared about her. But the most haunting part was that Anna hadn't even realized it until it was too late.

The last message from Sarah sat unread on her phone. It simply said, *I miss you, Anna. I hope you're okay. But I can't keep reaching out if you won't let me in.*

And in that moment, Anna understood the cruel truth: she had lost everything, not because of Sarah's betrayal, but because of Eliza's silent manipulation. And now, with no one left to turn to, she realized the extent of the isolation she had created.

The Fabricated Truth

Sophia had always been the one to hold the memories. She collected them like treasures—small moments of tenderness, words shared in secret, shared experiences that built the foundation of her life. She had always believed that a relationship was a living tapestry, where both people contributed to the narrative. But when she met Lisa, that tapestry began to unravel, thread by thread.

Lisa was magnetic. She had a way of drawing people in, of making them feel like they were the most important person in the world. At first, Sophia admired Lisa's confidence, her effortless charm, and the way she seemed to have everything under control. Lisa made Sophia feel like she had finally found someone who could truly understand her, someone who valued her.

But it didn't take long before the cracks started to show. The first sign was small. After an argument about something trivial, Lisa would say, "You know, I've always been the one to give, and I'm tired of it. You just don't appreciate me. You never listen when I need you."

Sophia, who had always been the one to give in relationships, would apologize immediately. It didn't matter that Lisa had been the one to raise her voice first, or that she had been dismissive. Sophia would apologize, again and again, until Lisa's mood softened. Lisa would smile, pull her close, and tell her it was okay, but the words didn't feel like comfort. They felt like a trap.

It wasn't long before Lisa started rewriting their shared history. Every argument, every moment of tension was suddenly cast in a new light. "You always do this," Lisa would say, looking at Sophia with pained eyes. "You never understand how much I've given up for us. Remember that time I had to cancel my plans to spend the evening with you? You just don't get it. I've sacrificed so much for this relationship."

Sophia would try to recall the memory, but all she could remember was the time she had waited patiently for Lisa to come home after a late meeting, the time she had made dinner for the two of them, the time she had quietly supported Lisa's ambitions, without asking for anything in return. But Lisa's version of events had begun to drown out her own.

At first, Sophia tried to protest, to correct Lisa, but each time, Lisa would look at her with those sad, wide eyes. "You don't remember, do you?" Lisa would whisper, her voice soft but carrying a weight that made Sophia's heart ache. "You never do. You always twist things, make me the bad one."

Sophia would feel the ground shift beneath her feet, like the familiar foundation of their relationship was being slowly eroded. She would tell herself that Lisa was just under stress, that maybe she was projecting. But each time, Lisa's version of events felt more real, and Sophia's own memories seemed to blur.

It was subtle at first, but then the gaslighting became more pronounced. Lisa would tell Sophia, "Remember when I supported you through your promotion? I was the one who believed in you. Without me, you wouldn't have even made it this far." Sophia's chest tightened. The truth was, it had been her own hard work, her sleepless nights, her dedication that had earned her that promotion. Lisa had been there, yes, but it was Sophia's effort that had made it possible. Yet, every time Lisa spoke about it, Sophia found herself doubting that reality. Maybe Lisa had been the one who had encouraged her. Maybe Lisa's support had been the turning point.

As the months passed, Sophia began to feel a growing unease. She had once been confident in her memories, in the truth she had lived, but now, the line between what was real and what was Lisa's version of the truth had begun to blur. Sophia started questioning herself. Had she really been as supportive as she remembered? Had she been neglecting Lisa's needs? Was she truly the partner she thought she was?

One day, as they sat in their living room, Lisa began recounting a trip they had taken together a year ago. "You were so selfish during that trip," Lisa said, her voice almost nostalgic. "I had to do everything myself. You never even offered to help when I was so exhausted. I spent the entire trip trying to hold things together, while you just did your own thing."

Sophia froze. The memory was so different in her mind. She had spent that trip trying to create perfect moments for them, cooking, planning little surprises, even giving Lisa space when she needed it. But Lisa's words twisted the entire experience into something unrecognizable. Sophia felt a lump rise in her throat. *Was I selfish? Did I really make her feel that way?*

"I don't think that's how it happened," Sophia said quietly, her voice trembling. "I thought we had a good time. I tried my best to make it special for us."

Lisa turned to her, her expression a mixture of pity and something darker. "You just don't remember, do you? You never do. You always make it about you. It's always about your needs, your happiness, your plans. I'm always the one who has to carry everything. But you wouldn't understand that. You never do."

The words hit Sophia like a punch. Her head spun. She didn't know what to believe anymore. Was she really the selfish one? Had Lisa really sacrificed so much for their relationship? Was she the problem?

Days passed, and the doubt only deepened. Sophia stopped talking to her friends, stopped reaching out to her family. She didn't want them to see how much she was unraveling. Lisa had already told her that they wouldn't understand. Lisa had already made it clear that they were the ones who had always been there for her, that she owed everything to them. And so, Sophia stayed quiet, lost in a fog of confusion.

It wasn't until months later, when Sophia was alone in their apartment after Lisa had gone to a meeting, that she finally found something—an old notebook of hers, tucked away in a drawer. As she flipped through the pages, her memories began to flood back. The moments that Lisa had twisted, the experiences she had stolen from her, all came rushing back. She remembered the sacrifices she had made, the love she had given. She remembered the truth. But it was too late. The damage had been done.

When Lisa returned, Sophia didn't say a word. She simply looked at her, the person who had manipulated her, who had rewritten their shared history, and realized the truth. She wasn't the one who had been lost. She was the one who had been stolen from.

The relationship was over, but the scars of the betrayal, the manipulation, would last far longer. Sophia realized that she had allowed herself to be trapped in someone else's narrative, to lose herself in someone else's version of the truth. And now, all she had left was the silence of her own broken reality.

The Weight of Silence

It was supposed to be simple. Natalie had always been the one to take care of things. She'd worked hard for everything she had, built a life from the ground up, and always prided herself on being independent. But when she met Sarah, something shifted. Sarah wasn't like anyone Natalie had ever known. She was sweet, sensitive, and had this way of making Natalie feel like she was the center of her world. She was always there, always ready to listen, to care. Natalie thought she had found someone who would understand her, someone who would bring balance to the chaos of her life.

At first, Sarah's emotional depth felt like a gift. She would listen intently when Natalie talked about her long days at work, her struggles with friends, her frustrations about the world. Sarah was supportive, compassionate, always ready with comforting words or a warm hug. "You're amazing," Sarah would say, her eyes filled with sincerity. "You deserve so much more than you're getting. I don't know how you keep going."

Natalie was touched, grateful for Sarah's attention. But soon, things began to shift. The support that had once felt like a refuge started to feel more like an obligation. One night, after a particularly long day, Natalie came home to find Sarah sitting on the couch, looking withdrawn.

"You're home late," Sarah said softly, her eyes downcast. "I was so worried about you. You never even called to let me know what time you'd be home. Don't you care about me? You know how I get when I don't hear from you."

Natalie froze, her heart sinking. "I'm sorry, Sarah. I didn't mean to make you worry. I just lost track of time."

But Sarah didn't smile. She didn't say it was okay. Instead, her voice took on a more fragile tone. "I just... I don't know how to deal with all this on my own. I feel so alone when you're gone. You're all I have, and sometimes it feels like you don't care enough to check in."

Natalie's stomach turned. She hadn't meant to make Sarah feel this way, but the guilt began to settle in, heavy and suffocating. She wasn't used to this. She was used to being the strong one, the one who helped everyone else. But now, it felt like she was being asked to carry more than just her own weight.

Over the next few weeks, Sarah's emotional needs began to consume more of Natalie's time and energy. It was subtle at first—small requests for reassurance, for extra attention—but soon, it became harder to ignore. Every time Natalie needed to focus on herself or her work, Sarah's voice would echo in her mind. "I just don't know how to cope without you. Please don't leave me to deal with this alone."

At first, Natalie tried to set boundaries, to tell Sarah that she needed time to recharge, to focus on her own life. But every time, Sarah would respond with quiet despair. "I don't know how I'm supposed to survive without you. I just need you, Natalie. I don't know what I'd do without you. Don't you understand? You're all I have left."

The guilt began to grow inside Natalie, each word from Sarah feeling like another weight on her shoulders. She had always been the dependable one, the one who could handle it all. But Sarah's dependence was different. It wasn't just about needing support—it was about needing Natalie to be responsible for her emotional well-being. And every time Natalie tried to pull away, Sarah's sadness and vulnerability made her feel like the worst person in the world.

One night, after a particularly exhausting week, Natalie tried to go out with friends. She hadn't seen them in ages, and she needed a break. But as soon as she stepped through the door that evening, she found Sarah sitting on the couch, her eyes red, tears streaking her face.

"You're going out again?" Sarah's voice was small, but the hurt was clear. "I thought you said you'd be here for me. I thought we were going to spend the evening together. But once again, you're choosing everyone else over me. I'm just not enough, am I?"

Natalie's heart twisted. She hadn't meant to hurt Sarah. She just wanted a night to herself, a break from the constant emotional toll. But instead, she found herself apologizing again, making excuses. "I'm sorry, Sarah. I just needed some time to clear my head. I didn't mean to make you feel this way."

Sarah's eyes filled with tears. "I just... I can't do this without you. I can't be alone with all these feelings. You don't understand how hard it is for me. I need you to stay, to be here. If you leave me now, I don't know what will happen to me."

The guilt tightened around Natalie's chest, suffocating her. She could hear the desperation in Sarah's voice, the helplessness, the overwhelming need. She had always been the one to help, to fix things. And in that moment, she couldn't bring herself to walk away. Instead, she stayed, sitting beside Sarah, the weight of her decision pressing down on her like an anchor. She had given up her night, her friends, her space—just to ease Sarah's pain.

But the truth, the painful truth, was that Sarah wasn't asking for help. She wasn't seeking support. She was manipulating Natalie, using guilt as a weapon to keep her tethered to her own emotional chaos. The more Sarah demanded, the more Natalie gave, and the more she lost herself in the process.

Days turned into weeks, and weeks into months. Natalie's world became smaller. Her work suffered, her relationships with friends deteriorated, and every moment of freedom was overshadowed by the constant guilt that came with trying to take time for herself. Every time she thought about leaving, about standing up for herself, Sarah's face would fill her mind—her pleading, her desperation, her sadness.

It wasn't until one evening, when Sarah once again needed her in the middle of a work deadline, that Natalie realized the truth. The truth wasn't about Sarah's neediness. It wasn't about Natalie's lack of support. The truth was that Natalie had allowed herself to be manipulated. She had allowed guilt to become the chain that kept her locked in a relationship where she was no longer herself.

"I'm sorry," Sarah whispered as Natalie sat by her, once again putting aside her own needs. But it wasn't Sarah who needed to apologize. It was Natalie.

And as the darkness of the evening closed in around her, Natalie realized that she was no longer just a partner to Sarah. She was a prisoner. The guilt had kept her there, and it had been slowly suffocating her.

But now, as the silence stretched, Natalie finally understood the cost of staying out of obligation. She had given up her life, her voice, and her identity—only to realize that the love she thought she was nurturing had been nothing more than a weapon used to control her.

The Mirror's Edge

Clara had always been a quiet soul, someone who felt more comfortable in the background. She'd never been the one to command attention in a room, and she had grown used to that. Her insecurities had always been there, lurking in the background like distant echoes she could never quite silence. Her body, her voice, her abilities—they all seemed to fall short compared to the people around her. She didn't mind it at first; it was just the way she was, and she learned to live with it.

Then, she met Emily.

Emily was everything Clara wasn't—confident, outgoing, and effortlessly magnetic. She drew people in without even trying, and when Emily set her eyes on Clara, it felt like the world had suddenly shifted. Clara had never felt so wanted, so seen, in all her life. Emily made her feel special, like she was worth something more than she had ever believed. In the early days, Emily would tell Clara how incredible she was—how intelligent, how beautiful, how rare. It was like Clara had finally found someone who could see through her self-doubt, someone who could pull her out of the shadows and make her feel like she mattered.

At first, it was intoxicating, a high she could never quite get enough of. Every compliment from Emily felt like a balm to her insecurities, soothing the parts of her she had spent years hiding. But slowly, things began to change. Emily's praise became more pointed, more targeted. "You know," Emily would say one night as they sat together, "if you just put a little more effort into your appearance, you'd really turn heads. You have a pretty face, but you don't dress like you care about it. It's like you don't want people to notice you."

Clara felt the familiar pang of insecurity, but she tried to laugh it off. "I don't know, I like being simple. It's just who I am."

Emily's eyes darkened for a moment, and then she softened, her voice gentle. "I just want you to be your best. People don't appreciate you the way you deserve. But I see it, Clara. You're worth more than you think."

Clara nodded, feeling the weight of those words pressing down on her. Emily wasn't wrong—she knew she wasn't as confident as the women around her. But Emily's approval had become like air to her now. She couldn't breathe without it. And so, she began to change, little by little. She started spending more time on her appearance, buying new clothes, trying to fit the mold that Emily seemed to want for her. Every time she made a change, Emily would notice, showering her with praise.

"You look so much better like this," Emily would say. "I can't believe you didn't dress like this before. See how good it feels?"

Clara began to feel a strange satisfaction in the changes. For the first time, she felt like she was gaining control over her life, like she was becoming the person Emily saw in her. But the satisfaction was fleeting, and Emily's demands began to escalate. "You should really work out more," Emily suggested one evening, her tone casual, but her eyes serious. "It'll make you feel stronger, more confident. I don't want you to feel bad about yourself anymore."

Clara hesitated. She wasn't unfit, but she wasn't athletic either. She had always avoided the gym, afraid of the way people would look at her. But now, Emily's words were like a command, and Clara found herself pushing harder than she had ever pushed before, running until her legs ached, lifting weights until her muscles burned. Each time she met Emily's expectations, the validation felt worth the exhaustion. But every compliment from Emily seemed to come with an unspoken weight—like the praise was a way to keep Clara tethered to her insecurities.

As Clara changed, so did the relationship. Emily began to subtly criticize the things she once admired. "You're doing so well with your fitness, but you still don't seem confident enough. Why are you always so shy when we go out? You know you should be enjoying yourself more. Don't you want people to see how amazing you are?" Emily's words cut deeper than Clara had expected. She was doing everything Emily asked—she was changing, becoming better, but still, it wasn't enough.

Clara started to feel like she was always chasing something that would never truly be within her reach. No matter how hard she worked, how much she gave, it wasn't enough to satisfy Emily's expectations. She became more and more dependent on Emily's approval, constantly seeking validation from her, feeling like she would collapse under the weight of the demands. Her life had shifted so much to meet Emily's needs that she didn't even recognize herself anymore.

One night, after another exhausting day of trying to meet Emily's ever-growing expectations, Clara finally snapped. "Why is it never enough?" she asked, her voice shaking with frustration. "Why do I have to keep changing? Why do I have to keep proving myself to you?"

Emily's expression softened, but only for a moment. She took Clara's hands in hers, looking deeply into her eyes. "I'm doing this because I care about you, Clara," she said, her voice low and soothing. "You have so much potential, but you're just not seeing it. I'm helping you become the person you're meant to be. You should be thanking me for making you realize how much more you can give. I'm the one who sees it. I'm the one who can make you better."

Clara's heart twisted. The words sounded so genuine, so full of love. But deep down, something inside her screamed. She had given up so much of herself—her comfort, her confidence, her ability to see her own worth. Emily had promised her more, but had only made her feel smaller, weaker, and more dependent on the validation that was always just out of reach.

The realization hit Clara like a ton of bricks: Emily didn't love her for who she was—she loved her for what she could be, for how much she could control. Every change, every adjustment to meet Emily's ever-growing standards, had been a way to keep Clara bound to her. It wasn't love. It was manipulation. Clara had become nothing more than a project, something to be molded into someone else's idea of perfection.

And as the weight of that truth settled in, Clara understood the price of her transformation. She had sacrificed her own sense of self, piece by piece, until all that was left was a shell, shaped by Emily's needs. She wasn't becoming the person she had always dreamed of being—she was becoming the person Emily demanded her to be.

Clara finally saw herself clearly, but by then, it was too late to turn back. She had already given away everything she had once been, and in the silence of the night, she understood the true cost of her dependency on someone else's approval.

The Price of Affection

Lena had always been the kind of person who craved love. Not just affection, but the kind of love that consumed, that promised a sense of belonging so deep it would fill every empty corner of her soul. She had never really experienced it in her past relationships—those were always the shallow, fleeting kind. But when she met Isabel, everything changed. Isabel was a different kind of presence. Charismatic, confident, and effortlessly charming, she seemed to give Lena all the attention and affection she had longed for.

At first, it felt like a dream. Isabel would surprise Lena with small gifts, whispered sweet nothings, and soft touches that lingered just a little too long. The kind of gestures that made Lena feel adored, like the center of someone's universe. Isabel would smile at her in a way that made her feel special, like no one else in the world mattered. "I don't know what I did before I met you," Isabel would say, her eyes full of warmth. "You're everything I need, Lena. You complete me."

Lena, starved for that kind of love, would bask in the glow of Isabel's words. She would do anything to keep the affection coming, anything to hold onto the connection they had. But soon, the affection came with strings attached.

It started with small requests—little things at first. "Can you skip dinner with your friends tonight? I really need you to be here with me," Isabel would say, her voice soft but firm. "I've had a tough day, and I just want to spend time with you."

Lena, feeling a flicker of discomfort but unwilling to challenge Isabel, would agree. After all, Isabel needed her. And the thought of losing that warmth, that affection, was too much to bear. So, she'd cancel her plans and spend the evening with Isabel, quietly pushing her own needs aside.

The requests grew more frequent, more insistent. Isabel would often downplay her own needs, making Lena feel like she was the one who had to step in, to be the strong one. "I can't handle things on my own today," Isabel would say, her voice fragile. "I need you to take care of me. I just want to know that you're here, that I'm not alone in this."

Each time, Lena complied. She made excuses to her friends and family, explaining that Isabel needed her, that Isabel was the priority. And as she did, Isabel would shower her with affection. "You're so amazing, Lena," Isabel would whisper, kissing her forehead. "I don't know what I'd do without you. You're the only one who truly understands me."

The affection felt like a drug—always just out of reach unless Lena did exactly what Isabel wanted. As the months passed, Lena found herself sacrificing more and more of herself, her time, her energy. She stopped seeing friends, stopped pursuing hobbies, stopped thinking about what made *her* happy, because it was easier to live in Isabel's world than to deal with the growing emptiness that was starting to gnaw at her.

Isabel's affection was the carrot, and Lena was the horse, always running after it, always chasing. If she did everything Isabel asked, if she molded herself into exactly what Isabel needed, the love would come. But the love always felt conditional, like a reward given only when Lena complied.

One night, after a particularly long week of catering to Isabel's needs, Lena finally spoke up. "I need some space, Isabel," she said, her voice shaking. "I haven't seen my friends in weeks, and I just need some time to recharge. I need to feel like *me* again, not just *us*."

Isabel's smile faltered for a moment, but then her eyes softened. She placed a gentle hand on Lena's cheek. "You're right," she said, her voice full of sweetness. "You're so right. You've been taking care of me so much. I'm just so scared of being alone. I don't know how to be without you."

Lena's heart sank, and she felt the pull of that affection once more.

"I don't want to hurt you," Lena whispered, guilt flooding her chest.

"No," Isabel said, a soft laugh escaping her lips, "you could never hurt me. You're everything I need. I just need to know that you won't leave me. I'm not strong without you. I don't want to feel abandoned."

Lena swallowed hard, her internal conflict eating at her. She didn't want to be abandoned either, didn't want to feel that emptiness again. And as she saw the vulnerability in Isabel's eyes, the affection returned, overwhelming her, suffocating her doubts.

"Okay," Lena said, her voice barely audible. "I'll stay. I'll be here."

Isabel's face lit up in that familiar smile, and Lena felt the weight of her decision settle into her bones. She had given up her life, her independence, all for the illusion of love. And as the days turned into weeks, that weight grew heavier.

But the manipulation never stopped. As Isabel's demands grew, the affection became more of a tool than a gift. Isabel would demand attention when it was convenient, and then pull away when it suited her. "I just don't think you care enough about me," Isabel would say when Lena tried to make plans or spend time on herself. "If you loved me, you wouldn't leave me alone like this. If you loved me, you would be here."

And each time, Lena would comply. She would drop everything, let go of her own needs, because the thought of losing Isabel's affection was unbearable. Each sacrifice was met with a kiss, a compliment, a reassurance. But it was never enough. Nothing was ever enough.

One evening, after Isabel had gone out with friends and Lena had stayed home waiting, the door clicked open, and Isabel walked in, her smile playful but calculating. "You've been waiting for me, haven't you?" she asked, her tone light.

Lena's stomach twisted. "I thought you needed me," she said quietly, her voice barely above a whisper. "You told me you couldn't be alone."

Isabel paused, her smile faltering for just a second. "Oh, I don't need you like that, Lena," she said, her voice shifting. "I just wanted you to feel like you were doing something for me. You've been so predictable. It's cute, but honestly, you're so easy to control."

Lena froze. The words hit her like a slap. *Easy to control.* She had spent months, no, years, running after Isabel's affection, doing everything she could to please her, to keep her close. And now, Isabel had admitted it—she had used Lena, manipulated her into staying, into giving, into sacrificing everything.

"I thought you loved me," Lena whispered, her heart breaking.

"I do," Isabel said, a smile playing at the corners of her lips. "But you love me more. That's what matters, right?"

Lena felt a sick realization settle in. The love she thought she had wasn't love at all. It had been a game—a game she had been playing with herself all along, one where the stakes were her self-worth, her identity, and her happiness. And she had lost.

Isabel's love had never been for Lena—it had only ever been for what Lena could give her.

The Illusion of Choice

Anna had always prided herself on being independent, capable, and in control of her life. She knew what she wanted, and she wasn't afraid to go after it. When she met Eliza, everything seemed to fall into place. Eliza was confident, sharp, and knew exactly what she wanted in life. Anna admired that, at first. She admired the way Eliza seemed to take charge of everything—how she always had a plan, a purpose. For someone like Anna, who often felt uncertain, Eliza's presence was a beacon, something solid and reliable.

At first, their relationship felt like an easy balance. Anna would bring her ideas and dreams to Eliza, and Eliza would offer her insight, her thoughts. "You're so much smarter than you think," Eliza would tell her, her voice smooth with praise. "You're capable of anything, Anna. You just need the right guidance."

Anna loved hearing that. She loved how Eliza made her feel important, how she always made sure to remind Anna that she was special. But as the weeks went by, Eliza's guidance turned into something else—something that felt less like support and more like control.

One evening, after a long conversation about Anna's future, Eliza casually asked, "So, have you thought about what you want to do with your career? You've been putting so much into it, but I feel like you're not really moving forward." Eliza's tone was gentle, but there was something underlying it—a quiet pressure that Anna couldn't quite put her finger on.

"I'm not sure," Anna admitted. "I guess I've been a little stuck. I want to keep growing, but I don't know how."

Eliza smiled, a warm, reassuring smile that made Anna feel like she was safe. "Well, I think you have two choices," Eliza said, her voice calm, thoughtful. "You could either take that big promotion that's been offered to you in your current job, or you could take a step back, move somewhere quieter, and focus on your personal life for a while. Both options could work for you, but it depends on what's more important to you right now."

Anna felt the weight of the decision suddenly pressing down on her. The promotion was tempting, but it would mean more stress, more responsibility. The idea of stepping back sounded appealing too, but it would mean giving up on the hard work she had put in to get where she was. The choices felt difficult, but in the back of her mind, she trusted Eliza. After all, Eliza had always been the one with the answers.

"I don't know," Anna said after a pause. "Both choices sound good, but they're so different. What do you think I should do?"

Eliza leaned forward, her hand resting gently on Anna's. "I think you should take the promotion," she said softly. "You've worked so hard to get there, and I know you can handle it. But if you feel overwhelmed, you can always adjust later. You'll be fine."

Anna nodded, though a small voice inside her still had doubts. The promotion felt like it came with an invisible weight, and she wasn't sure if she was ready for it. But Eliza's reassurances calmed her fears, and she convinced herself that this was the right path. The next day, Anna accepted the promotion, feeling a small sense of pride mixed with a growing uncertainty that she couldn't shake.

As the months went by, the pressure of the promotion became heavier. Long hours, endless meetings, and the constant stress began to take a toll on Anna. She had less and less time for herself, for her friends, and for the things she used to enjoy. But every time she expressed her concern, Eliza would remind her that this was what she had chosen.

"You're doing great," Eliza would say, running her fingers through Anna's hair, soothing her. "You made the right decision. You have so much potential, Anna. I'm so proud of you for not giving up."

But as the weight of her responsibilities grew, Anna started to feel more and more alone. She couldn't remember the last time she had a moment to breathe, to relax, to just be. She was always working, always pushing forward, always striving to meet Eliza's expectations. And when Anna tried to question her decisions, when she tried to express her frustrations, Eliza would always have the answers.

"You know, you're just overthinking it," Eliza would say. "You're doing so well. You just need to push through. You don't want to give up now, do you? You don't want to disappoint everyone who believes in you."

The pressure continued to build, and Anna's life began to feel like a constant cycle of exhaustion and self-doubt. She tried to reach out to her friends, but the distance between them felt wider than ever. The moments she used to cherish seemed lost, replaced by late nights at the office and endless discussions with Eliza about what was best for her.

One evening, after yet another grueling day at work, Anna finally broke down. "I can't do this anymore, Eliza," she said, her voice trembling. "I feel like I'm losing myself. I feel like I'm doing everything for you, for this job, and I don't know what's left for me. I don't know what I want anymore."

Eliza's face softened with concern, but Anna could see the calculation in her eyes. "I know you're tired, Anna. I know you're feeling overwhelmed," she said, her voice full of sympathy. "But you've come so far. You can't just walk away from everything you've worked for. I'm here for you. You know I only want what's best for you."

But as Eliza spoke, Anna began to realize something—a terrifying truth that had been creeping up on her for months. Every decision she had made, every path she had chosen, had been framed by Eliza's influence, her manipulation. The choices had never been her own. Eliza had presented her with "choices," but in reality, each one had been carefully crafted to serve Eliza's agenda, to keep Anna in a place where she was always striving for validation, always striving for more.

Anna had never truly made a choice. She had simply followed the paths Eliza had laid out for her, convinced that the love and attention she received from Eliza were worth the cost.

And as that realization settled in, Anna understood the full extent of the manipulation. Eliza hadn't been supporting her. She had been controlling her, shaping her life to fit her own desires, and using the illusion of choice to make Anna believe that everything she did was her own decision.

But it was too late. Anna was already trapped—caught in the illusion that love and validation could only come if she followed Eliza's lead. The choices had never been hers to make, and now, as she looked at Eliza's calm, satisfied expression, she knew that she would never escape the web of control she had woven around her.

The Space Between Us

Eliza was everything to Maya. From the moment they met, there was an instant connection, a bond that seemed to fit perfectly. She was charming, confident, and carried herself with a magnetic energy that made Maya feel like she was the most important person in the room whenever they were together. Eliza would make small gestures—attentive, thoughtful, always focused on Maya. In those early months, it felt like a dream, a beautiful whirlwind of affection and intimacy. Eliza had a way of making Maya feel understood, like no one had ever truly cared for her before.

But slowly, as the days turned into weeks, something began to shift. Eliza began to raise small, seemingly innocent comments about Maya's friends, her family, and the people closest to her. "Do you really think Sarah has your best interests at heart?" Eliza asked one night, the question lingering like smoke in the air. "I mean, she's always been so independent. Don't you think she's trying to make you more like her?"

Maya, who had known Sarah for years, was taken aback. "What do you mean? She's just my friend, Eliza. She supports me."

Eliza smiled, but there was something in her eyes—a knowing look that made Maya uncomfortable. "It's just that I see how much she pulls you away from me. She doesn't really understand us, Maya. I think she wants you all to herself."

Maya dismissed it at first, thinking Eliza was just being protective, maybe a little insecure. After all, Sarah had always been a strong presence in her life, someone she trusted deeply. But the more Eliza spoke, the more doubt crept into Maya's mind. She started to notice how Sarah's casual plans would sometimes clash with Eliza's needs. Whenever Maya made time for Sarah, Eliza would pout, or worse, make her feel guilty.

One night, after a long conversation about work and life, Eliza asked, "Do you think your mom really understands how much pressure you're under? I mean, she's always asking for your time, but you're so busy, Maya. Don't you think she's asking too much from you?"

Maya was confused. "She's my mom, Eliza. She's always been there for me. I want to make time for her."

"I know," Eliza said gently, "but don't you think she's being selfish? I mean, you have to choose. You can't keep giving everyone else pieces of yourself and still have something left for me. I just don't think she sees how much you're struggling. How much *we're* struggling."

The guilt settled deep in Maya's chest. She began questioning everything—the phone calls with her mom, the weekends she spent with friends. Slowly, without even realizing it, Eliza had created a wedge between Maya and the people she cared about most. Maya found herself canceling plans with Sarah, making excuses not to visit her mom. Eliza always seemed to be waiting, needing her, and the more Maya gave, the more Eliza demanded.

The tension between them escalated. Maya started feeling suffocated, torn between her life before Eliza and her life with her. Whenever Maya tried to reach out to anyone else, Eliza would get quiet, distant, and Maya would feel the sting of guilt. "I don't want to make you choose," Eliza would say, her voice soft but insistent, "but I just don't think you realize how much it hurts when you spend more time with other people than with me. I need you, Maya. I thought you understood that."

Maya would apologize, again and again, convincing herself that she was being unfair. That Eliza needed her more. That maybe her friends and family didn't understand the weight of the relationship, the depth of the connection they shared. It wasn't that she didn't care about them—it was that Eliza made her feel like she was betraying something sacred by giving time to anyone else.

As weeks passed, Maya began to distance herself more from her friends and family, the people who had once been her support system. Her world became smaller and smaller, and she convinced herself it was for the best. But deep down, a part of her knew something was wrong. She felt trapped, caught in a cycle of guilt and sacrifice. And still, Eliza's affection, her attention, was always the prize, the reward for doing exactly as she was told.

One evening, after an argument with her mother over a missed dinner, Maya sat in their apartment, her head spinning. Eliza, as always, was there to comfort her, to soothe the guilt and shame that simmered under the surface. She held Maya close, whispering soothing words, reminding her how much she cared.

"You're mine," Eliza whispered. "You don't need anyone else. I love you more than anyone could ever understand."

Maya felt a moment of relief—Eliza's warmth, her affection, felt like everything she had been searching for. But as she pulled away, something in her snapped. She looked at Eliza, really looked at her for the first time, and the truth hit her like a freight train.

"I don't even see Sarah anymore," Maya said, her voice shaking. "I've cut off my friends, my family... and for what? For you. But now I'm losing myself. I've pushed everyone away because of you. You've made me feel guilty every time I wanted to spend time with anyone but you."

Eliza's eyes darkened, and for the first time, Maya saw a flicker of something cold. "I'm just trying to help you see what's important," Eliza said softly, but her tone was sharp. "You were always so distracted, so concerned with everyone else's needs. I'm just helping you focus on us, Maya. On *me*. I thought you'd understand that."

Maya felt the walls close in around her. The affection, the warmth—it had all been a manipulation, a way to make her feel like she owed everything to Eliza. The choices, the sacrifices, the guilt—they had all been engineered to serve Eliza's needs.

Maya stood, backing away from Eliza, feeling the suffocating weight of realization. "You've turned me into someone I don't recognize," she whispered.

Eliza stood, too, her face unreadable. "It's not my fault," she said, her voice strangely calm. "You made the choice to be with me. I've given you everything."

Maya looked at her, the love that once felt all-consuming now just a weapon used to manipulate her. She had sacrificed her entire support system—her friends, her family—for the illusion of a love that was never truly hers. She had been played, and now, standing in the silence of the apartment, she understood the truth.

Eliza had never wanted her to be free. She had only wanted her to be dependent. And now, with no one left to turn to, Maya was completely alone.

The divide had been created, not by anyone else, but by the one person who had promised to love her.

The Price of Praise

Sophia had always been cautious about love. She had been burned before, let down by promises that never came true, and was determined not to make the same mistake again. But then, she met Miranda.

Miranda was different from anyone Sophia had ever known. She was captivating, effortlessly charming, and had an energy that made you feel like the world was better just for being in her presence. Every word Miranda spoke seemed perfectly timed, every glance charged with meaning. It didn't take long for Sophia to fall under her spell. Miranda made her feel beautiful, special, and unique—like she was the only one in the room. Sophia had never experienced this kind of attention before, and it felt like everything she had longed for was finally within her reach.

"You're incredible, Sophia," Miranda would say, her eyes alight with admiration. "I can't believe someone like you is real. You're so intelligent, so beautiful, so kind. I just feel so lucky to be with you."

Sophia, starved for validation, soaked in Miranda's praise. It was exactly what she needed to hear—words that made her feel seen, wanted, appreciated. And the more Miranda praised her, the more Sophia wanted to please her. She would do anything for that kind of attention, for that kind of love.

At first, the praise was flattering. It made Sophia feel like the best version of herself. Miranda would compliment her appearance, her work, her intelligence. "You're so much smarter than people give you credit for," Miranda would say, her voice gentle but insistent. "You could do anything you set your mind to, Sophia. You're exceptional, and everyone should know that."

Sophia felt her confidence grow, swelling under the weight of these compliments. Miranda was right. She *was* exceptional. She was worthy of all this attention, of all this love. But as time passed, the compliments began to shift, becoming less about Sophia's qualities and more about her willingness to please Miranda.

"You know," Miranda would say with a playful smile, "you don't always have to be so guarded. I think it would be so much better if you just let go, trusted me a little more. You're perfect, but I think you could be even more perfect if you let me in fully. Don't you want to be the best version of yourself for me?"

Sophia, eager for Miranda's approval, didn't think much of it at first. After all, Miranda had always been supportive, always made her feel like she was enough. What harm could there be in trusting Miranda a little more? So, little by little, she let her guard down. She stopped saying no to Miranda's requests, stopped setting boundaries, and began giving more of herself than she ever had before.

But the more she gave, the more Miranda seemed to want. "You're amazing, Sophia, but I think you could be doing more," Miranda would say, a hint of disappointment in her voice. "You know, I just feel like you hold back sometimes. You're so talented, but I don't think you push yourself enough. I know you can be better for me. I just want to see you shine, fully."

The words were like a drug to Sophia. Every compliment, every hint of approval made her feel validated, made her feel like she was finally worthy. Miranda had a way of making everything sound so reasonable, so loving. "I just want the best for you," Miranda would say, her hand gently brushing Sophia's cheek. "But to be the best, you have to give me everything. No more holding back. You owe it to yourself, and to me."

Sophia began to lose herself in Miranda's desires. She found herself constantly trying to live up to Miranda's expectations, constantly striving for more approval, for more praise. She began to believe that the only way to be loved, to be appreciated, was to abandon her own needs and bend to Miranda's will. She gave up her hobbies, her friends, her sense of self, because she was convinced that if she just pleased Miranda enough, she would finally be *enough*.

As the weeks went by, the manipulation grew more insidious. "You're incredible," Miranda would whisper, wrapping her arms around Sophia, "but don't you think you should be spending more time with me? You're always so busy with other people, and I don't feel like I get enough of you. I want you to be here, with me, all the time."

Sophia tried to explain, tried to tell Miranda that she needed time for herself, that she couldn't give up everything. But Miranda's face would fall, and she would look at Sophia with those sad, pleading eyes. "I just want you to care about me the way I care about you. I'm here for you, but I feel like you're always thinking of others first. Don't I deserve to be your priority? You say you love me, but if you love me, you would put me first. Why can't you just trust me fully?"

The guilt was overwhelming. Every time Miranda would manipulate Sophia with those soft, sad words, Sophia would feel like the worst person in the world. She would cancel plans with friends, stay in when she needed to recharge, all to avoid making Miranda upset. The approval, the praise, was worth the sacrifice. It had to be.

But as time went on, the affection that had once felt like a treasure became a cage. Miranda's praise, once so genuine, now felt like a tool—a tool to make Sophia feel indebted, to make her believe that the only way to keep Miranda's love was to keep sacrificing herself. Sophia's boundaries had been worn down to nothing. She had no identity left beyond Miranda's expectations.

One night, as Sophia lay awake in their bed, Miranda beside her, she realized the depth of her own loss. She had given everything, all for the illusion of love, all for the promise that if she did enough, she would finally be worthy. But in doing so, she had lost herself entirely.

The woman who had once known what she wanted, who had once had her own dreams, was gone—replaced by someone who existed only to please Miranda.

When she tried to speak, to voice her feelings, Miranda's smile was the same as always—sweet, warm, and filled with affection. "You're amazing, Sophia. You really are," Miranda said softly. "But I think you're just afraid of how perfect you could be. I just want to help you be better. You deserve to be everything I know you can be."

Sophia looked at her, and for the first time, she saw the manipulation behind the praise. She saw how Miranda's love had always come with a price, how it had always been conditional, how it had always been about what Sophia could give, not who she was. And yet, as Miranda's hand rested gently on hers, Sophia couldn't bring herself to walk away. The praise, the affection, had worn her down to the point where she couldn't imagine a life without it.

The twisted truth hit her like a cold wave. She had been loved into submission, and now, there was no escape.

Under the Surface

Chloe had always been independent. She worked hard, paid her bills on time, and managed her own life without much help from anyone. She had a small group of friends she trusted, a job she loved, and a life that, while modest, was hers. That was, until she met Emma.

Emma was everything Chloe wasn't—charismatic, confident, and seemingly perfect. When they first started dating, Chloe was swept off her feet. Emma was attentive, affectionate, and filled with compliments that made Chloe feel like she was finally seen. "You're incredible, Chloe," Emma would say, her voice warm and adoring. "You deserve someone who'll take care of you, make sure you have everything you need. I just want to help you, make your life easier."

Chloe, who had always prided herself on doing everything on her own, was hesitant at first. But Emma's constant reassurance, her promises of making things better, felt like a relief. It wasn't long before Chloe found herself giving in. It started with small things—Emma helping her with a few bills, managing the grocery list, scheduling Chloe's doctor's appointments. Chloe, feeling overwhelmed by work and life, didn't mind. Emma seemed genuinely interested in making her life easier. She was only trying to help, right?

But as the months passed, Emma's "help" became more pervasive, more controlling. It wasn't just the bills anymore. "I noticed you've been spending a lot at that coffee shop lately," Emma said one evening, her tone casual but her eyes focused. "I think you should start brewing your own coffee at home. It's cheaper, and I know you're always worried about money."

Chloe blinked, unsure how to respond. "It's just a small indulgence, Emma. It's not a big deal."

Emma smiled sweetly, but Chloe could see the hint of disapproval in her eyes. "It's not about the coffee, Chloe. It's about being smart with your money. I'm just looking out for you, you know? I want you to be able to save, to not worry. We need to make sure you're thinking long-term."

Over time, Chloe began to feel like her decisions weren't really her own anymore. Emma would insist on managing Chloe's time, setting up every appointment, scheduling social outings, and even deciding what Chloe should wear for events. At first, Chloe didn't mind. It felt like Emma was simply being thoughtful, taking some of the pressure off her. But soon, it felt suffocating. Chloe wasn't making decisions anymore. Emma was.

"You don't need to meet with Sarah this weekend," Emma said one evening. "I've already made plans for us, and you've been so stressed lately. I think we should just have a quiet night in instead."

Chloe tried to protest. "But Sarah's my best friend, Emma. We've been planning this for weeks."

Emma's expression softened, and she placed a hand on Chloe's shoulder. "I know, sweetheart. But I really think you need some time to relax. You're always going, going, going. I'm just trying to take care of you. You don't want to burn out, do you?"

Chloe hesitated, but the guilt crept in. She didn't want to disappoint Emma. Besides, maybe she *did* need the rest. Emma had always been right about everything else.

Slowly, Chloe's world shrank. She stopped seeing her friends as much, stopped making decisions for herself. Emma seemed to always know what was best for Chloe, and Chloe couldn't help but trust her. It was easier to just let Emma handle everything—after all, Emma had proven she could make things better.

But things started to feel off. Chloe would open her bank statements and see large withdrawals that Emma had made. "I noticed you've been going over budget this month," Emma said, a touch of concern in her voice. "Don't worry, I transferred some money to cover it. We just need to be a little more careful next time."

Chloe, unable to keep track of where the money was going, trusted Emma. She didn't want to rock the boat. "Okay," she said quietly, trying to ignore the unease bubbling in her chest. "Thanks, Emma."

It wasn't just the finances that Emma controlled anymore. Chloe found herself avoiding plans with her friends, telling them she was too tired or that Emma had already planned something else for them. "I'm sorry, Sarah," she said on one such occasion. "Emma wants to stay in tonight. Maybe next time."

She hadn't realized how much of her life Emma had taken over until one evening, when Chloe stumbled upon an email from Emma's work, mistakenly opened on their shared laptop. It was a request for Emma to take over Chloe's financial accounts—something that Chloe had never agreed to. Her heart pounded in her chest as she read through the email: "Please review the attached budget proposal for your partner, Chloe. I've noted several opportunities for investment that I believe will benefit you both."

Chloe felt the ground shift beneath her. Her stomach twisted with the realization—Emma had taken full control, manipulating Chloe into giving up her own boundaries under the guise of "helping." Her finances were being controlled. Her social calendar was controlled. Even her personal choices, her friends, her time—everything was being shaped by Emma's decisions.

Chloe confronted Emma, her voice trembling. "Why did you do this? Why didn't you tell me? Why are you making all these decisions for me?"

Emma looked at her with those same sweet eyes, the same calm, comforting smile. "I'm just trying to protect you, Chloe. You have so much potential, but you're always so distracted by the little things. You're always so worried. Let me take care of the big stuff. You're too precious to be weighed down by these small details."

But Chloe could see it now—the manipulation beneath the praise, the control hidden in every act of "care." Emma had never wanted to make Chloe's life better. She had wanted to take it over. She had wrapped Chloe in a web of dependency, made her believe that without Emma's guidance, she would be lost.

Chloe's heart sank as the full weight of what had happened hit her. The choice had never been hers. Emma had made sure of that. And now, Chloe realized too late that the life she had been living was no longer her own.

Emma leaned in, cupping Chloe's face gently. "I'm only doing this because I love you. You're mine, Chloe. You'll see that, eventually. You don't need anyone else."

And for the first time, Chloe realized just how much she had lost.

Under Her Thumb

Mara had always been the type of person to stand on her own two feet. She was driven, passionate about her work, and fiercely independent. She prided herself on making decisions without needing validation from anyone else. That was, until she met Lily.

Lily was unlike anyone Mara had ever encountered. She had an air of confidence that seemed almost effortless. The way she spoke, the way she carried herself—it was magnetic. Mara, who had never really let anyone in too close, found herself drawn to Lily, wanting to be part of her world. Lily, in turn, showered Mara with attention, lavishing her with compliments and praise that made her feel seen in a way she hadn't before.

"You're amazing, Mara," Lily would say with a smile that lit up her whole face. "You have so much potential. You just need someone who believes in you. I can help you get there."

Mara, starved for affirmation, soaked in Lily's words. It felt good to be wanted, to be needed. At first, it was all harmless. Lily was supportive, encouraging, always quick to praise Mara's accomplishments. But slowly, as their relationship deepened, Mara began to notice something subtle—something off about the way Lily's "support" worked.

It started with little comments, things that, on the surface, seemed like advice. "You've done well with this project, Mara," Lily would say, her voice sweet and soothing, "but I think you're overthinking it. You need to trust your instincts more. Let me help you streamline it, so it can really shine. You don't have to do everything on your own."

At first, Mara didn't think much of it. Lily was just trying to help, right? But over time, it became clear that Lily's help came with strings attached. Mara would second-guess her decisions, feeling like she needed Lily's approval to move forward with anything. The more Mara relied on Lily's guidance, the more she began to doubt her own instincts.

One day, after Mara had taken the initiative to handle a situation at work, Lily's reaction took her by surprise. "I mean, it wasn't *terrible*," Lily said, her tone light but critical. "But I would have done it differently. I think you might have made it harder than it needed to be."

The words stung more than they should have. Mara had put in a lot of effort, and yet, instead of praise, Lily had found a way to undermine her confidence. "I was just trying something new," Mara said, feeling defensive.

"I know," Lily replied, a soft chuckle in her voice. "But sometimes, you need someone with more experience to show you the right way. You know, I've been through a lot of situations like this before. You could really learn from me, Mara. I'm just trying to help you avoid the same mistakes."

The way Lily said it made Mara feel small. It wasn't that Lily was being overtly harsh, but the constant subtle undermining had begun to take its toll. She started questioning herself more. Her decisions became less about what *she* wanted and more about what Lily thought was best. Lily's "help" was making her feel less capable, less confident in her own abilities, until Mara started to believe that she couldn't trust herself without Lily's approval.

This pattern continued to grow. With every step Mara took, Lily was there, offering her support but always subtly directing it. When Mara bought a new dress, Lily would say, "You look great, but I think you should have chosen something with a little more color. That's what works for you, trust me."

When Mara decided to take on a new project at work, Lily would smile and say, "I'm glad you're branching out, but you'll need my help. You don't want to make the same mistakes you made last time. I've been in your shoes before, remember? You just have to listen to me."

Mara started feeling trapped in a world where her choices were never truly her own. Every decision she made was tainted by the thought of whether Lily would approve or not. She felt like a puppet, with Lily as the strings holding her in place, always in the background, always guiding her, always needing her to need her.

One night, Mara decided to finally confront Lily. She was tired, exhausted by the constant pressure of needing approval for every little thing. "Lily, why do you always feel the need to take over everything?" she asked, her voice trembling with frustration. "I want to make my own choices. Why can't you just let me do things on my own? I'm capable of handling my life."

Lily's expression softened, almost as if she hadn't expected the question. She stepped closer to Mara, gently brushing a lock of hair behind her ear. "I know you are, darling. But I'm just here to help you become the best version of yourself. You don't have to do it all alone. You shouldn't have to make those mistakes. I want to see you succeed, and sometimes, that means I need to step in. You trust me, don't you?"

Mara's heart skipped a beat. There it was again—the familiar pull, the reassurance that everything would be okay if she just let Lily in. It wasn't that Lily was ever malicious; she was always so caring, so gentle, with just the right amount of praise to make Mara feel like she was the one in control. But the truth was, Lily's "help" had gradually become her leash.

"You *do* trust me, right?" Lily repeated, her voice a little softer now, but with an underlying pressure.

Mara nodded, almost automatically. She had been conditioned, molded into a version of herself that couldn't function without Lily's approval. "Yes, of course. I trust you."

Lily smiled, her eyes gleaming with a satisfaction that made Mara shiver. "Good. Because I just want what's best for you, Mara. I'm always here to help. You're never alone."

But in that moment, Mara realized that she had already given everything up. The illusion of choice, the idea that she was in control of her life, was just that—an illusion. Lily had wrapped her in a web of well-intentioned manipulation, and now, Mara was stuck in a life that wasn't really hers anymore.

The approval had come at a cost. It had cost her her independence, her sense of self. And as Lily leaned in to kiss her, Mara realized, with a chilling clarity, that she had traded her autonomy for the comfort of never having to make a decision again.

The Race to Nowhere

Claire had always prided herself on being the best. Whether it was at work, at home, or even in her friendships, she strived for excellence. It wasn't that she sought approval—at least, not in the traditional sense—but the feeling of surpassing expectations gave her a sense of security. It made her feel powerful. That was how she had always operated—until she met Ava.

Ava was charming, confident, and always just a little more than Claire could ever be. She was the kind of person who walked into a room and commanded attention. There was no doubt that she was captivating, and Claire found herself captivated, too. At first, it felt like a breath of fresh air. Ava seemed to have it all together, effortlessly breezing through life. But as their relationship grew, so did the tension.

At first, it was subtle—a comment here and there, like when they went out for dinner and Ava casually remarked, "You're always so late with decisions, Claire. I'd be done by now." Claire would laugh it off, thinking it was just Ava's sense of humor. But soon, it became clear that everything was a competition, and Ava was always the victor.

"You should really start taking your health more seriously," Ava said one morning, watching Claire sip her coffee. "I mean, I've been eating clean for weeks now, and I feel amazing. Why don't you try it? You'd be surprised at what you can accomplish if you really push yourself."

Claire, always the one to be in control of her choices, was unsettled by the comment. She wasn't unhealthy; she simply didn't adhere to the strict diet Ava did. But Ava's tone made Claire feel like she was falling short, like she was being lazy, weak. "Maybe I'll try," Claire said, her voice hesitant. The thought of being seen as incapable, or of being less than Ava, was too much. She didn't want to appear like she was failing, especially when Ava made everything seem so effortless.

Every conversation seemed to morph into a comparison—whether it was about how fast Claire could finish her work or how little time she took to relax. "You're always working, Claire. I thought you had more time for *us*, but I guess I'll just have to keep up with my own schedule," Ava would say with a soft sigh, leaving Claire feeling like she was neglecting her relationship even when she tried her hardest to balance everything.

The feeling of always falling short, of always needing to do more to satisfy Ava, was starting to eat away at Claire. She had become a person who made decisions only to avoid criticism, who sought Ava's approval in every aspect of her life, from how she dressed to how she interacted with friends. Every choice was analyzed through the lens of whether it would please Ava.

One night, as they sat on the couch, Claire brought up a work opportunity that had been offered to her. "They're giving me the chance to head the new project," Claire said, her voice excited. "I think it's a big step for me. I'm not sure if I should take it yet, though. It's a lot of pressure."

Ava smiled, but there was something cold behind her eyes. "Of course you should take it," she said, her voice almost too sweet. "But don't forget to prioritize your time. It's important to maintain balance, you know? You wouldn't want to end up like those people who work themselves into the ground."

Claire nodded, still unsure. But Ava's words made her feel like there was no other option—like she was making a mistake by even considering anything other than Ava's advice. After all, Ava's life appeared so perfectly curated, so effortlessly successful. It was clear to Claire that Ava always knew what was best, and so she accepted the opportunity, knowing it would please Ava.

Days turned into weeks, and Claire's life became a blur of work, trying to meet Ava's expectations, and then striving to fix the mistakes Ava pointed out. Every success felt less like her own and more like something she had to prove, to show Ava she was capable. But no matter what Claire did, it never seemed to be enough.

"You always think you're doing enough, Claire," Ava would say. "But really, you should be further along by now. You've wasted so much time trying to make everything perfect when you should've been focused on your priorities."

The weight of Ava's words crushed Claire, but she didn't know how to escape. How could she, when every step she took was shadowed by Ava's criticism and her praise in equal measure? Ava always made Claire feel like she was failing but never in a way that was outright malicious. No, Ava's manipulation was far subtler—like a quiet hum in Claire's mind that grew louder with every passing day.

One afternoon, after Claire had spent hours on a project to meet Ava's standards, Ava looked at her with that same tired smile. "You've worked so hard, but there's still so much you could've done better," she said, not with malice, but with a gentle tone that made Claire feel small. "I think you could really benefit from working smarter, not harder, like I do."

Claire didn't know how to respond. Her entire life had become about working harder, about keeping up with Ava. But Ava's tone always made her feel like no matter what she did, it would never be enough. She felt like she was chasing something that would always be just out of reach.

Then one day, after weeks of constant pressure and strain, Claire broke. She had pushed herself to her limit, trying to keep up with the expectations that Ava had set for her. She had sacrificed her friendships, her peace of mind, and her sense of self—all for the approval of someone who would never let her truly succeed.

"I can't do this anymore," Claire finally said one evening, her voice shaking. "I've done everything you've asked. But I'm not me anymore. I've lost myself trying to please you."

Ava looked at her, a knowing smile on her face. "You were always so easy to control, Claire," she said softly, almost fondly. "I knew you'd come around. You're just like the others. Always trying to outdo me, but never quite getting there. You've made it so easy for me to guide you."

The coldness in Ava's words hit Claire with a brutal force. She had never been a partner in this relationship. She had never been valued for her own choices. She had been molded into someone who existed solely to compete with Ava, someone who was always wrong, always less than, always striving for a perfection that Ava dictated.

And in that moment, Claire understood that the competition had never been about her improving. It had always been about her failing.

The Weight of Her Care

Maggie had always been a bit reserved. She wasn't the type to easily open up or share her emotions, but that had never bothered her. She was content with the small circle of friends she had, content with her work, and content with the quiet peace that came from a life that didn't demand much. That was, until she met Naomi.

Naomi was everything Maggie wasn't—warm, outgoing, and full of energy. She was the kind of person who walked into a room and immediately drew people in. Maggie found herself mesmerized by Naomi's charm, the way she seemed to effortlessly connect with others. Naomi had a way of making Maggie feel like the center of attention, like she mattered in a way she hadn't felt before. Every time they were together, Naomi's compliments and gestures made Maggie feel seen in a way that felt almost too good to be true.

"You're such a good person, Maggie," Naomi would say, her voice soft but filled with sincerity. "You deserve someone who will take care of you, someone who will always be there for you. I want to make sure you have everything you need."

Maggie felt a wave of relief wash over her. Naomi's words were comforting in a way she hadn't realized she needed. She had never been one to ask for help, but Naomi made it feel natural. She wanted to take care of Maggie, wanted to make her life easier. "I've got you," Naomi would say, with that reassuring smile. "I'll always be here for you."

In the beginning, Naomi's support felt like a gift. She would offer to help with Maggie's errands, give her advice when she seemed unsure, and show up with flowers or small thoughtful gifts. Maggie began to feel like Naomi was someone she could rely on, someone who understood her in a way no one else ever had. But over time, Naomi's "help" started to feel more like an obligation.

At first, Maggie didn't notice how subtle Naomi's manipulation was. It was disguised as kindness, as selflessness. Naomi always framed her actions as being for Maggie's benefit, always putting Maggie's needs above her own. "You're so tired, Maggie. You've been working so hard. Let me handle dinner tonight. You don't need to worry about anything."

Maggie, grateful for Naomi's gestures, would accept, feeling a bit guilty for not being able to reciprocate. "You've done so much already," she'd say. "I don't know how to thank you."

Naomi would brush it off with a laugh. "Don't worry about it. I want to do this for you. You deserve it."

But slowly, Maggie began to realize that the more Naomi did for her, the less Maggie did for herself. Naomi insisted on planning their social events, picking the places they went, even deciding how Maggie spent her free time. Whenever Maggie made a suggestion, Naomi would gently, but firmly, steer her toward something else.

"Are you sure you want to go to that party with Sarah?" Naomi asked one evening. "I don't think she's really your friend. She doesn't appreciate how much you've done for her. Maybe you should just stay in with me tonight. You know I'd love to spend more time with you."

Maggie, who had known Sarah for years, felt a pang of guilt. "I don't know, Naomi. I was thinking of going, but... you're right. I should spend more time with you."

Naomi smiled, but there was something cold behind it. "I just don't want you to waste time on people who don't value you. You deserve more than that, Maggie."

It was small things like that—Naomi subtly questioning Maggie's relationships with her friends and family, suggesting they weren't worth her time, making her feel guilty for considering spending time away from her—until Maggie began to pull away from those relationships. Naomi had made her feel like her world should revolve around Naomi and Naomi's needs. And, somehow, Maggie didn't even realize when it had happened. Naomi had made her feel so special, so appreciated, that Maggie started to believe Naomi was the only one who truly cared about her.

One night, Maggie came home after a long day at work, to find Naomi waiting for her with dinner prepared. She was tired, emotionally drained, and just wanted to relax. But Naomi, as always, was there, smiling and eager to take care of her.

"You've had a rough day, haven't you?" Naomi said, sitting beside her on the couch, her hand gently touching Maggie's arm. "You don't have to do anything tonight. Let me handle everything. You've worked so hard, you deserve to be pampered."

Maggie nodded, grateful but also overwhelmed. "I don't know what I'd do without you," she said, her voice almost a whisper.

Naomi's smile widened. "That's what I'm here for. I love taking care of you. I love making your life easier."

The words felt comforting, but a small voice inside Maggie's mind began to stir. Something didn't feel right. Naomi's constant care, her constant attention—it was beginning to feel suffocating. Naomi always made her feel like she couldn't live without her, like she was too fragile to function without her help.

The next day, after Naomi had gone to work, Maggie found herself staring at the blank pages of a notebook, wondering what she wanted for herself. Naomi had taken over every part of her life—her schedule, her time, her decisions. She was always there, always "helping," always guiding. But Maggie had stopped making her own choices, stopped thinking for herself. She had become so reliant on Naomi's approval that she didn't know who she was anymore.

Maggie began to feel a deep unease, a sense of loss. She hadn't asked for help—at least, not in the way Naomi had given it. She hadn't asked to lose herself, to become so dependent on Naomi's approval. But now, every action she took felt calculated to please Naomi. She no longer knew what she wanted outside of Naomi's approval.

When Naomi came home that evening, Maggie didn't say anything at first. She simply stared at her, a growing realization in her chest. Naomi was looking at her with that familiar smile, as if nothing had changed. "Are you okay, love?" Naomi asked, her voice sweet, but her eyes sharp.

Maggie's heart pounded. "I don't know who I am anymore, Naomi. I've lost myself in trying to please you."

Naomi's smile faltered for a moment, but then it returned, colder, more calculating. "You're just tired, Maggie. You've been working so hard, and I'm just trying to help you. I've been here for you. I love you. Don't you want me to take care of you?"

The words hung in the air, thick with expectation. And in that moment, Maggie realized the truth. Naomi wasn't taking care of her. Naomi had been taking everything from her. Her independence, her confidence, her relationships—they had all been sacrificed in the name of Naomi's so-called "help."

And as Maggie looked into Naomi's eyes, she knew the real cost of kindness was always manipulation.

The Illusion of Love

Sophie had never been one to jump into relationships easily. She had always valued her independence, and the idea of giving up her own life to blend into someone else's had always felt like a trap. That was, until she met Julia.

Julia was everything Sophie had never known she wanted. She was warm, attentive, and immediately made Sophie feel like the center of the universe. On their first date, Julia had gone all out—an intimate candlelit dinner at a cozy restaurant with a breathtaking view of the city, followed by a walk under the stars. Sophie had never experienced anything like it. Julia spoke with such ease and sincerity, making Sophie feel like they had known each other for years, not just hours.

"You deserve someone who treats you like royalty," Julia had said that evening, gazing at Sophie with a look that made her heart race. "I'm going to show you a love you've never known."

Sophie had smiled, feeling a warmth spread through her chest. For once, someone was treating her the way she had always dreamed of being treated. Julia was attentive to every detail—always complimenting her, always asking how she was feeling, always showing her that she mattered.

The honeymoon phase lasted for weeks. Julia continued to shower Sophie with affection—surprise gifts, thoughtful notes, spontaneous adventures. Every day seemed like a new chapter in a fairy tale, and Sophie found herself falling harder and harder. Julia's gestures were too perfect, too ideal to be true. Sophie felt like the luckiest woman alive.

But as the days passed and Sophie became more emotionally invested, things began to change—slowly, at first, but in a way Sophie couldn't ignore. The affection from Julia began to come with expectations. One evening, after Sophie had finished a long day at work, she came home to find Julia waiting with dinner, a smile on her face.

"You know, I was thinking about how much we've been spending on dinners lately," Julia said, casually pushing the plate of food toward Sophie. "I don't think it's necessary to keep going out like we have been. It would be better if we started saving. For us. For our future."

Sophie paused, unsure of what to say. "I've been working hard, Julia. I like treating myself every now and then."

Julia's smile faltered for a moment, then softened. "I get it, I do. But you don't need to treat yourself with money, Sophie. The way I see it, we should be focused on building something together. Don't you think that's more important?"

Sophie nodded, feeling a small knot form in her stomach. "Yeah, maybe you're right."

From then on, Julia started subtly pushing Sophie's boundaries. At first, it was little things—suggesting Sophie spend less time with her friends, telling her it would be better if she focused more on "their relationship." Sophie began to pull away from the people she had once confided in. Julia had a way of making her feel guilty for not prioritizing her, for not giving her undivided attention. Every time Sophie tried to hold onto a piece of her old life, Julia would make her feel like she was neglecting the relationship.

"You know, it doesn't seem like you're giving me the same attention as you did when we first started," Julia had said one evening, her voice soft but laced with something darker. "I thought we were building something special, but lately, I feel like I'm not your priority. Maybe I was wrong to expect more from you."

Sophie immediately apologized, her stomach twisting with guilt. "I'm sorry. I didn't mean to make you feel that way."

Julia smiled, but it didn't quite reach her eyes. "It's okay. I just want you to be more aware of how much I'm doing for us. For you. I'm just trying to make sure we have a future together, Sophie."

As the days passed, Julia's words began to seep into Sophie's mind, and every time she made a choice, she found herself asking: *What would Julia think of this?* It was no longer about Sophie's needs or desires—it was about what Julia expected, what Julia wanted. Sophie found herself constantly adjusting her behavior to meet Julia's standards, constantly seeking Julia's approval.

The final shift came one night, when Julia made a decision without consulting Sophie. They had planned to spend the evening together, but Sophie had an important deadline to meet at work. Julia, however, had made plans for the two of them to attend a party, and when Sophie tried to explain that she needed to work, Julia's reaction was swift and cold.

"You've been working too much lately," Julia said, her tone clipped. "I thought you were someone who could balance work and love. Clearly, I was wrong."

Sophie felt the sting of the words, but before she could respond, Julia continued. "I've been trying so hard to make this work, Sophie. But if you can't prioritize our relationship, I don't know how much longer I can do this."

The guilt was overwhelming, suffocating. Sophie agreed to go to the party, putting aside her work and her own needs yet again to please Julia. When they arrived, Julia clung to her the entire night, refusing to let Sophie speak to anyone else. Sophie felt trapped, unable to even enjoy the night, her thoughts consumed by Julia's disapproving gaze every time she tried to talk to a friend.

By the time they returned home, Sophie was exhausted, emotionally drained. Julia, however, was wide awake, sitting on the couch with a glass of wine, staring at Sophie with a look that seemed too calm, too calculating.

"I just want you to understand something, Sophie," Julia said, her voice low but firm. "I'm not asking for a lot. I've given you everything, and I've tried to be patient. But I need you to choose me, and only me. You can't have both, and if you want this to work, you need to stop living for everyone else."

Sophie stood there, the weight of Julia's words crushing her. She felt suffocated, as though the walls were closing in around her, and for the first time, she realized the truth. The love she had thought was perfect had been a carefully constructed illusion. Julia's affection, her gestures, her idealized romance—it had all been a trap, a way to draw Sophie in and make her feel obligated to comply with every demand.

Sophie had been manipulated from the start. Every romantic gesture, every compliment, had been a tool to control her, to make her give up her independence and submit to Julia's vision of their life. And now that Sophie was emotionally invested, Julia had no reason to hide her true intentions anymore.

Sophie's heart sank as the realization hit her. She had been so blinded by love, by the idea of the perfect relationship, that she had failed to see the manipulation until it was too late.

The Empty Promises

Grace had always been afraid of being alone. She didn't remember exactly when it started, but as far back as she could remember, the thought of abandonment had clung to her like a shadow, a constant undercurrent in every relationship she had ever been in. Her family, though loving, had always been distant in their own way, and Grace had learned to compensate for it by being overly accommodating, constantly adjusting herself to fit others' needs. She gave too much, said yes too often, and in the end, felt invisible in her own life.

When she met Mia, everything changed. Mia was magnetic, the kind of person who effortlessly made people feel seen, like she was the answer to their every question. When Mia smiled at Grace, it felt like the world tilted on its axis. Mia's words were soft but carried an intensity that made Grace feel important. She was patient, caring, and made Grace feel as though she had never truly been loved until now. Mia was always there when Grace needed her, her support unwavering.

"I just don't think anyone could love me like you do," Grace would say, overwhelmed with the attention, the care.

"I would never leave you, Grace," Mia would reply with that smile that always put Grace at ease. "You are everything to me. I'll always be here. You don't have to worry about that."

It was the reassurance Grace had craved for so long, the thing she had been searching for her whole life. The feeling of not being alone. And for a while, she believed it.

But as the days passed, small cracks began to show in Mia's perfect facade. It started when Mia began to distance herself, little by little. She would cancel plans at the last minute, or disappear for hours without explanation. The first time Grace confronted her, Mia responded coolly, "I was just tired, Grace. I don't think you understand how much pressure I'm under. But I'm here now. You have me, don't you?"

Grace, anxious and unsure, nodded. "Of course. I just—I don't know. It's just been hard."

Mia's face softened instantly, like a storm clearing. "I know, babe. I know. You don't have to worry. I'm not going anywhere. But you have to understand, sometimes I need my space too. It's not you. It's just me."

The reassurance felt familiar, like a comforting blanket. But that blanket was becoming heavier. The space Mia needed was becoming more frequent, and Grace found herself walking on eggshells. Every moment she spent alone felt like a crack in their relationship, a fissure that might grow if she didn't hold on tightly enough.

As the months passed, Mia's absence became more pronounced, but every time Grace questioned her, Mia was there to soothe her fears. "Why are you worried? Don't you know how much I care about you?" Mia would say, her voice gentle but firm. "I'm not going to leave you. But you have to trust me. You have to trust that I'll always come back."

Grace, terrified of the possibility of being left behind, always complied. Mia's words were like a balm to her fears, but they also slowly chipped away at her sense of independence, her ability to function without Mia's constant affirmation.

Then came the silences. Mia would go days without answering Grace's texts or calls, but whenever Grace reached out in desperation, Mia would return with just enough care to calm her down. "Sorry, I was busy. You know how it is. But I'm here now. Don't ever think I've forgotten about you."

Grace began to feel like she was losing herself. Mia's presence was her lifeline, and every absence, every moment of distance, sent her spiraling into panic. She started to believe that if she didn't behave a certain way—if she didn't constantly prove how much she needed Mia—she would lose her for good.

One night, after Mia had gone silent for an entire weekend, Grace finally snapped. "Where have you been? I've been worried sick. You can't just ignore me like that."

Mia's response was cool and measured, almost too perfect. "Grace, you have to stop being so needy. You know that I love you. I told you, I won't leave. But you're suffocating me with your constant need for reassurance. I need space. You need to trust me."

The words hit like a slap, but Grace didn't have the strength to push back. Instead, she apologized, begging Mia to understand how scared she was. "I just need you," she said, her voice trembling. "I need to know you won't leave me."

Mia's eyes softened, and she moved closer, cupping Grace's face gently. "I won't leave you, Grace. You just have to trust me. But you can't keep demanding my time. You have to let me breathe."

The tears fell freely from Grace's eyes, but this time, they weren't from relief. They were from the realization that she had been manipulated all along. Mia had fed her every insecurity, every fear of abandonment, until Grace no longer knew how to function without her approval. She was no longer a person in her own right—she was an extension of Mia's need to control, to keep Grace clinging to her like a lifeline. Every gesture of love had come with a cost. Every word of reassurance had been a manipulation.

Mia leaned in, kissing Grace softly on the forehead. "I love you," she whispered. "You're everything to me. But you need to trust me more."

And in that moment, Grace understood the dark truth: Mia's love had always been conditional, and her fear of abandonment had been the perfect tool to control her. Mia had never truly been there for her—she had only been there to keep Grace dependent, afraid of losing what she had never truly owned.

As the days passed, the cycle continued. Mia would pull away, and Grace would beg for reassurance. And every time, Mia would come back, just enough to keep Grace from breaking, but always leaving her wanting more. Each time, Grace felt the hollowness inside her grow, until one day, she realized she was no longer waiting for Mia to come back.

She was waiting for herself to leave.

The Cost of Love

Maya had always believed in love as something pure, something that could never be quantified. To her, love was about connection, trust, and shared moments of vulnerability. But all of that began to change when she met Veronica.

Veronica was unlike anyone Maya had ever met—charming, charismatic, and magnetic in a way that made everyone around her feel important. At first, she was everything Maya had ever wanted. Veronica was attentive, generous with her affection, and always made Maya feel like she was the center of her world. She would send texts throughout the day, little thoughtful gestures that made Maya feel cherished. They would talk for hours, and Veronica would often remind Maya how lucky she was to have found someone like her.

"You're incredible, Maya," Veronica would say, her voice soft but insistent. "I don't know how I've managed to go this long without someone like you. You make my life complete. You deserve so much, and I want to give it to you."

Maya soaked in the praise. It was everything she had ever longed for—a relationship where she wasn't just a side note, but the most important part of someone's life. And for the first few months, it was perfect. Maya believed in Veronica's sincerity, and the attention she was receiving felt like a validation of her worth.

But as their relationship deepened, Veronica's needs began to surface, and they were never small. It started with simple requests—asking Maya to skip a dinner with friends to spend more time with her, saying that she just needed a little more support at home, or that she was feeling down and needed Maya to cheer her up.

"I don't want you to think I'm being selfish," Veronica would say after making one of these requests, her voice pleading. "But I just need you, Maya. I don't know what I'd do without you. You're all I have, and sometimes, it just feels like I'm not getting enough from you. You know how much I care about you, right?"

Maya would always agree, of course. How could she not? Veronica made it sound like a reasonable request—like it was Maya's duty to show her love through actions, through giving. The first few times, Maya didn't mind at all. In fact, it felt good to be needed, to feel that her love could make such a tangible difference in someone's life.

But the requests kept coming, and they began to grow in intensity. Soon, Maya was canceling plans, putting her own needs aside, and spending more and more time trying to meet Veronica's expectations. Veronica, it seemed, always had a new need. She would ask Maya to take care of things Veronica herself had neglected—anything from picking up groceries to handling complicated situations at work, all under the guise of love and care.

One evening, after Maya had spent hours helping Veronica with a project that wasn't even her responsibility, Veronica looked at her with that familiar smile and said, "You're so good to me, Maya. I don't know how I could survive without you. But I need to ask for something else. I know this might sound a little selfish, but it's important. I need you to be more present for me. I feel like I'm doing all the emotional labor in this relationship, and I can't do it alone anymore. I need you to meet me halfway."

Maya felt the familiar knot of guilt tighten in her chest. *She was doing everything she could,* and yet it never seemed to be enough. She wasn't getting anything in return, but the weight of Veronica's words made her feel as though she was failing her. She promised herself that she would do better, that she would give more.

The days turned into weeks, and the emotional weight of Veronica's increasing demands began to suffocate Maya. She stopped seeing her friends, stopped taking care of herself. Veronica needed her, and Maya couldn't stand the thought of being the one who let her down. But the more Maya gave, the less Veronica seemed satisfied.

One day, after Maya had spent the entire day running errands and helping Veronica with various personal issues, Veronica casually remarked, "You know, I've been thinking about how much I give you, and I don't think I'm getting as much in return. You haven't been as affectionate with me lately, and I feel like I'm the one doing all the emotional work here."

Maya felt a cold wave of panic wash over her. She had done everything Veronica asked. She had sacrificed her own happiness, her own well-being, in the name of love. And yet, Veronica was accusing her of not doing enough. It was like nothing she did could ever meet Veronica's ever-growing needs.

"You've been a little distant," Veronica continued, her voice quieter now, almost accusatory. "I feel like I'm always the one giving. I'm always the one who makes sure you feel loved, but I don't always feel that from you."

Maya's throat tightened, and she swallowed hard, trying to push back the tears that threatened to spill. "I'm sorry," she said, her voice barely above a whisper. "I've just been trying to take care of you, and I don't know how to do it all. I don't know how to be everything you need."

Veronica stepped closer, her hands gently cupping Maya's face. "I know you're trying, Maya. But love is a transaction. I give, you give. If I'm the one always giving, I need you to meet me halfway. If you want me to keep loving you, you have to do the same."

The words hung in the air, suffocating Maya. The realization hit her like a slap in the face. Love was no longer something freely given—it had become a series of transactions, each one with increasing demands.

Veronica had turned affection into something she could *earn*, something she had to *work* for, and now, she was made to feel guilty for not doing enough.

"I just need you to try harder, okay?" Veronica said softly, as if consoling a child. "I'm not asking for much. I'm just asking for what I deserve."

Maya nodded numbly, her mind reeling. She had given so much of herself to this relationship, but all she had received in return was guilt, manipulation, and the constant pressure to do more, be more. But the hardest part was the realization that she was caught in a cycle she didn't know how to escape. She had already given so much of herself that she wasn't sure who she was anymore.

That night, as she lay in bed beside Veronica, she felt an overwhelming emptiness. Veronica's steady breathing beside her only highlighted the silence in Maya's heart. She had spent so much time giving, so much time trying to fill the void between them, that she had lost herself in the process. The love that she had once thought was a gift now felt like a weight. It had never been a gift at all. It had been a transaction, a demand disguised as affection.

Maya knew then that she was trapped, unable to give enough to fill Veronica's insatiable need, and too far gone to realize where the love for herself had gone.

Get Another Book Free

We love writing and have produced many books.

As a thank you for being one of our amazing readers, we'd like to offer you a free book.

To claim this limited-time offer, visit the site below and enter your name and email address.

You'll receive one of our great books directly to your email, completely free!

https://free.copypeople.com

Also by Morgan B. Blake

The Hidden Truth
Silent Obsession

Standalone
Temporal Havoc
The AI Resurrection
99942 Apophis
The Shadows We Keep
Whispers of the Forgotten
Christmas Chronicles: Enchanted Stories for the Holiday Season
Realm of Enchantment Tales from the Mystic Lands
The Taniwha's Secret
Unicorn Magic Discovering the Wonders of a Hidden World
Vampire's Vow: Stories of Blood and Betrayal
Legends of the Damned: Villains Who Defied Fate and Conquered All
Twisted Affection: How Love Can Break You